ENJOY!
Flora Doone

OAF

By Flora Doone

OAF

A novel by Flora Doone.

First printing 2018.

All rights reserved.

Copyright November 2018

ISBN-13: 978-1729811764

Cover Design

Flora Doone

For Mallory who I love to the moon and back again.

For Wes who believed in my writing from the start.

For the amazing critique group I am honored to be a part of.

For the court jesters who are my guardian angels.

By Flora Doone

When I walk, the earth shakes. No, I mean it –
everything shakes. Sometimes I try to hold my breath,
thinking that it might make a difference, that my rolls of flesh
will tighten and stay in one place, but really, who am I
kidding?

I speed up, managing to make it to science class
seconds before the bell rings and into the lab where nobody
wants to be my partner. Feeling their eyes follow me to the
closet where the one-size-doesn't-fit-all lab jackets hang, I grab

the nearest white coat, toss it over my shoulders and make my way to the table in the far corner where Candy Sapperstein pretends not to see me coming. She won me in a pick-a-partner, coin toss lottery.

"Hey, Candy." I fake a smile and sit. The stool whines under the pressure of my two hundred and ninety-five pound ass. My bloated, stubby fingers make an attempt at being delicate with the glass slide I'm trying to handle.

"Here, Rick, I'll do it." Candy slips a fingernail under the slide and places it beneath the clips of the microscope. I watch as she lowers her eye to the eyepiece, squeezing the other eye shut, cracking her gum. I wish I had a piece of gum.

Candy's hair falls across her face and sweeps the desk with every turn of her head. She slides the microscope my way and makes notes on her lab sheet. We're looking at the inside of Candy's cheek. Mine would gross her out so I just didn't offer the day we swabbed.

"Mr. Balentine, would you tell us what your findings are about this specific tissue?" Mr. Hartman is always putting me on the spot. But here's the thing of it. If I answer, then people look at me, and that means my face goes all red, and then the worst part – sweat. As much as I'd like to disappear, be invisible, I can't. See, there's two things everyone knows about me, it's that I'm about as smart as I am fat. And while I wouldn't mind being invisible, in some way I like everyone knowing just how smart I really am.

"I'm waiting," Hartman taps the marker against the white board.

"Cheek cells do not move on their own..." I clear my throat, "so you will not find two organelles that function for cell movement." I wipe the small beads of sweat forming on my upper lip.

Candy scribbles on her notebook and pushes it toward me. It's got a stick figure with a round circle for a body, fat fingers sticking out with no arms and the words *Rick = Brainkenstein* written next to it. Sometimes I wonder how she made it to AP Science.

I shrug at Candy's attempt at being a caricaturist, cross out *Brainkenstein* and scribble in *Sapperstein*, draw on a set of boobs and an arrow pointing directly at her.

"Ewwwwww." She cringes.

"Gum, Candy?" Hartman starts to walk toward our table when she sticks her gum on the corner of her lab sheet and folds up the end. I'm a little grossed out. Hartman, however, is satisfied and walks back to the board.

"Mr. Balentine," Hartman turns and looks at me. "Keeping in mind that the mouth is the first site of chemical digestion in a human, your saliva starts the process of breaking down the food you eat. What organelle do *you* think would be numerous inside the cells of *your* mouth?" He crosses his arms over his chest. "I know you have the answer."

Hartman calls on me when nobody else raises their hand, but this time, just this once I would appreciate him not calling on me to answer a question about where the process of breaking down food begins. I feel my face grow hot and stare out the window. This time I don't answer. I watch two Emo chicks slip through the hole in the fence and out toward *Java Jungle*. It's where all the kids hang out when they're cutting classes. I've never been.

The bell rings and I try to lose myself in the throng of students, which is generally impossible because wherever I am people tend to move away. Jockstraps are walking toward me and all I can think is *here I go again*. Sure enough, The Mighty Oak passes me, but not before butting his shoulder against mine, sending me careening into a cluster of non-entities only to be noticed now because of me. I can't tell if they're embarrassed for me or just embarrassed. I look at the three girls I've known since grade school and whisper I'm sorry. They have the good fortune of going unnoticed. Nobody picks on them, nobody bothers them. They're just fixtures around the school.

I move back into the crowd, head down, and out the

door of Beckett High. Unfortunately for me I live close by, too close. I live so close that you can see the athletic field from my kitchen window – a skinny God's joke – only I have to walk around the entire school to get to my block. A car tears down the street, turns around and follows me.

"Hey, lardass!"

At this point in my experience-rich life, I know I shouldn't look up, but I do anyway, and the moment my eyes meet the driver's he yells, "Now!" Two full moons shine from the car window as they speed away.

"How original," I whisper to my not-so-guardian angels, and decide to cut through the athletic field to my street after all. I don't usually take this shortcut in case the Jockstraps are practicing, but it seems their choice in sports today is drag racing and mocking me. Game over.

***

There's a delivery guy hauling boxes to my front door. Another of Mom's *House Beautiful Shopping Network* purchases – another thing to add to Dad's small list of arsenals to use against her.

"Nobody's home," the delivery guy says, handing me an *etch-a-sketch* to sign. "I rang the bell and there was no answer."

"Duh," I say, fishing for my key. I take the packages from him, balance them on my knee and unlock the door. There's already a stack of boxes lining the foyer of the house. I add these to it, go back and get the rest, dumping them near the door so Mom knows her shipment is in.

In the kitchen, my after school routine begins with a liter bottle of Pepsi, of which I drink about a third and fill the rest with milk. Pepsi milk has got to be the best invention since the egg cream. The egg cream was the best invention until I discovered Pepsi milk. An egg cream was something my grandmother used to make me. She'd claim the ingredients were imported from Brooklyn: chocolate syrup, seltzer, milk and a raw egg from a Brooklyn chicken. My grandmother refused to stop using raw eggs when salmonella became a risk for food poisoning. "Am I dead?" she'd say. Then she would go into a great diatribe about how you could defrost meat on the counter overnight and not die from that *e-cauliflower* disease.

On the table, next to two cans of onion soup is a note from Mom telling me to pour the soup over a hunk of meat in the fridge and to put it in the oven at five o'clock. This is the extent of her cooking. Usually, it's a weekly trip to Chef Mark's where you choose off a menu of meals, put the ingredients together in plastic boxes and bags, take them home and pretend you've cooked the meal yourself. If she could order her meals from the *House Beautiful Shopping Network*, she would. Instead, she has Chef Mark, and me, her son, forced to cook like the daughter she never had.

Whipping up a tasty snack is next on the agenda, as I make myself a few triple-decker peanut butter, banana and jelly sandwiches, grab a bag of chips and head downstairs to the cloister that is my room. I used to have the whole basement, but now there are boxes of canned foods infringing on my space. Mom thinks we'll be more prepared than the neighbors in the event of nuclear fallout, swine flu or a terrorist attack because we have canned peaches. I don't think she's ever considered putting a can opener down here. What a rude awakening that will be!

The basement is my haven. I moved in after my grandmother died. They had a bedroom and bathroom built for her and a living area with a kitchenette, which is now stacked with boxes, but the rest of it's mine. To look at the couch, you'd think someone should throw it out and maybe get a new one, but I rescued it before Mom sent it to the shelter. Now it's got a scoop at one end that my butt finds perfect for watching TV.

Parking myself, I plant my afternoon snack on the end

table and put my feet up on a carton of canned figs that I sure as hell will never eat. Homework can wait. I never struggle through homework. I can usually polish it off in half an hour.

My routine continues as my fingers command the remote and wait for the signal to take hold. Dr. Phil is handing someone a tissue and telling them it is okay to cry. I'm riveted. I wait to find out what could possibly be wrong today. It seems her fiancé has asked her to try things to fulfill his fantasy and that she's tried them but doesn't want to do them anymore and the fiancé has made it a condition of their marriage. Dr. Phil says leave him, there are other fish in the sea. I go to take another bite of a sandwich and it's gone. I didn't even realize I was eating. I down the rest of my Pepsi milk and flip through the channels, settling on a rerun of *Law & Order*. Now here's a show that really insults your intelligence. DNA in a day? Who are they kidding?

Upstairs I rifle through the mail. There's a Weight Watchers magazine in the pile. Mom thinks if I read the magazine I'll get some pointers on how to shed those *extra* pounds. When I was twelve, the doctor told her to take me to the meetings but she wouldn't. She was afraid people might see her a failure as a mother, letting her child get so fat. She never told Dad that she didn't take me. We'd go shopping instead. Dad usually blamed Mom for my weight, insisting that it was her fault. We won't go into the secret trips to the ice cream store where instead of going for the non-fat soft serve, Dad let them serve me up a triple scoop, triple topping sundae. "Don't tell your mother," he'd wink.

At five, I take the roast out of the refrigerator, pour the soup over the meat and vegetables, and stick it in the oven. Mom will turn it off when she gets home, whenever that will be.

The light on the phone pulsates, like it's trying to send out a message in code. I check messages on the off-chance someone's calling to tell me I've won a trip to Hershey, Pennsylvania and a lifetime of chocolate bars.

"Are you there? Aunt Helen, it's Dylan –"

My cousin. Oh, why bother. Messages are never for me. I go to hit the number "9" for save, only I nearly drop the phone and in my attempt to save the receiver, hit "7" with my dumb ass big thumb, erasing the message. Mom's gonna freak.

Jockstraps yelling plays on the athletic field pull me toward the window. I can see The Mighty Oak running sideways, hugging a football. He wouldn't be so mighty if people called him by his first name, Oswald. I only know that from our grade school days where he was kind of whiny. We went to different middle schools which must be where he stopped whining, shot up like a tree and got the nickname. That had to be it. He stood six-foot-two with a solid build at only sixteen. Me, I'm a not-so-solid five seven and instead of shooting upward in middle school I shot outward. If I had my choice of brains versus brawn, I think I'd choose the later.

Whenever Oak's around, I find myself watching him – not like I'm gay or anything, but sometimes I can't take my eyes off of him. Like when he's outside playing football or hanging with a bunch of people, the way they're drawn to him like he's some kind of god. He flashes a grin and the girls look away as if they're too shy to handle it. He takes it all in, smiling like he's a real good guy. What I would give to smile and make a girl shudder. Any girl! Even the fat girls won't look at me.

The sun is starting to set and that only means one thing, get my homework done because tomorrow is another day of school, another day of having to deal with all those people. I'm thinking of throwing myself a pity party but who would come? Instead, I check out the *blog du jour*, one a fellow fat kid writes. There's more to us than meets the eye.

FAT_vs_FICTION@BLOGSLOP.COM

Photos of me: 0

Profile: Round

Friends: 0

PAST BLOGS:

Fat vs. Fiction

Meaty Fingers

French Fries
in Paradise

Judging the
Outer Shell

Who Wants
Seconds?

Guilt

*Click here
for more...*

LEAN & MEAN

Is one synonymous with the other?

At my school, it seems like the guys who are "fit" will treat you like crap. I know, you wanted me to rhyme there, but I won't descend to their level. I've got to have some dignity.

And while we're on the subject of dignity, do you think there's any dignity in being a person of, let's say, the larger stature? Since I started this blog, all the other fat kids out there are telling me their stories. I know you feel alone but heck, there are tons of us (no pun intended).

I'm here to tell you YOU ARE NOT ALONE!

Look, I could have started any blog and being anonymous and all, I could have said I was thin, muscular, and really good looking. But I didn't! I let it all hang out because you don't know me. You don't know who I am, where I live or what I do. Heck, you might even think I'm a girl – I'm not, by the way.

Face it. We love to eat. And what are we gonna do about it? How many diets have you tried? I tried them all and I last about three days. It's no use.

I was thinking about what it would be to starve. I mean, if your body goes into starvation mode, it starts to eat away at all your stored fat. Imagine how long we could actually live without eating. If we were stuck on a desert island with no food, we might all survive! Actually, we'd probably wind up cannibals. Never mind.

Back to lean and mean. How do you get these guys to back off? How do you let them know that the ridicule could scar you for life? (Read that somewhere.) Like, do they even have a clue what it is to be us? They're not like us, so why is it we're the ones who are different?

Start a movement! Let's stage a huge rally with all the fat kids in the country and march the Mall in Washington, D.C. and let them know who we really are!

Any volunteers?

47 comments

Will there be snacks? Count me in!

Chapter 2

"Are you sure these still fit?" Mom pulls my gym uniform from a pile of laundry.

"Yeah, as much as anything fits." I grab the uniform and stuff it into my backpack. I can't believe I even have to wear this thing.

"Take socks," she yells.

Dad walks in, holding the phone. His face is grim and he won't look Mom in the eye. "It's for you." He sits down and watches her.

"Yes? Oh, no." Mom puts her head in her hands and rocks back and forth. Dad takes the phone from her and with one hand on her shoulder finishes the conversation.

"Sure, of course we will. No, no problem at all." Dad hangs up the phone, takes a deep breath and looks at Mom. "Well, we knew this was coming."

"What's coming? What's going on?" I look at Mom, then at Dad, but nobody is looking at me.

"Your Aunt Diane is gone." Mom's voice cracks and she sobs into Dad's shirt. "I just spoke with her two days ago."

"Oh, I forgot, Dylan called yesterday." I feel like an idiot, not giving Mom the message. "I totally spaced out, sorry. The answering machine –"

Mom gets out of her grief just long enough to hiss. "That's using your head, Ricky. You forgot? You know calls like that are important!"

Sorry isn't going to cut it just about now but I say it anyway. "Sorry."

"I know...I'm sorry I snapped." Mom isn't really the type to yell and make it stick.

My Aunt Diane has been dying for a long time. The big "C". Mom's two other sisters and her own mother all died from breast cancer. Mom had the test and they didn't find any genes at risk so she feels all this survivor's guilt at being the only one. Aunt Diane and Mom made a plan that if and when she died, Dylan, her son, would come to live with our family.

I can't tell Mom and Dad that I'm not so keen on the idea of having someone come live with us. Sure I feel bad for Mom, losing her sister and all, and for my cousin Dylan, but what's it going to do to *my* family? Besides, I'm used to this only child deal. Another person in the picture might just mess up what I've got going on here in my extra-ordinary world.

Dad sits next to me and puts his hand on mine as if to comfort me. I don't need comforting. I don't really feel anything that I guess I'm supposed to feel.

"I don't really know Dylan that well," I say to Dad, quietly so Mom can't hear me.

"What do you mean, he's your cousin," he whispers back as if this has great meaning. "He's family, after all." Dad runs a hand across the stubble on his face.

"Dad, we see each other every few years at some family thing, not like we've ever spent any real time together. I think I was like twelve the last time I saw him."

Dylan, a few months older than me, was always the one under the table at those big parties, drinking rum and coke and smoking cigarettes with my other cousins. I was the one lying on the carpet with only my head under the tablecloth and the rest of me under someone's chair. Now Dylan was coming to live with us, in my old room, upstairs with my parents. Good luck with that.

Dad drives me to school, even though it's only around the corner. He wants to take this opportunity to have a talk.

"Listen, things are going to be a little strange around here at first, with your cousin Dilly coming to live with us."

"Dilly? Isn't he too old to be called Dilly?" I shift the weight of my backpack and feel around, making sure my lunch is there.

"Don't get smart with me. This is just what I'm talking about. Dylan isn't like you." Dad pulls over before reaching the school, the car still running. He puts a hand on my shoulder and gives me a fatherly squeeze. "Dylan just lost his mother, have some compassion."

"Dad, I didn't say anything!" The car was warm, too warm. I could feel the perspiration under my arms start to soak my shirt. "I know Dylan is different than me. Everyone is different than me. Are you going to have this same talk with him? Tell him to treat me like anyone else?" I open the zipper to my jacket and tug at the collar of my shirt and say what Dad wants to hear. "I'll treat Dylan just like he was my own brother."

"That's all I'm asking," Dad smiles and puts the car into gear. He drops me off in front of the school and I walk like Moses to the steps while the crowd parts for me. *I'm not a leper.*

***

Today is Friday and first period is Phys Ed, which I'm

excused from but Coach Mart the Fart makes me get into my uniform and sit on the side lines. "Maybe you can learn something," he always says. I figure I can teach them something, like jock itch is actually a common fungus called *Trichophyton rubrum*, the very same fungus that infects the toes, like athletes foot. Do they want to learn that?

As fate would have it, my locker is artfully stuck between two of the most popular Jockstraps in the school. I wait until everyone is out of the locker room before putting on my gym shorts and gym shirt. The material is hardly breathable and my thighs chafe when I walk. It's a living hell every time I have to put this suit on and even more so when I walk to the bleachers. The class is in full force by the time I make my way out to the gym.

The sound of sneakers skidding on a wooden floor gives me as much of a thrill as eating eggshells, and the ball bouncing and echoes of boys in heat are enough to make me want to throw up. I look at the clock. Only forty-nine minutes, fifteen seconds and probably a few nanoseconds left to P.E. I watch the hand move slowly around and around, drowning out any sounds and think about the change coming to my house. Maybe it won't be so bad having *someone* around, someone to hang out with, play video games, maybe even go to the movies with. I indulge myself with the thought that this

Dylan thing might have possibilities.

"Ball!" The Fart yells as it sails over my head and winds up behind me on the bleachers. "*Ball,* Balentine!"

The game stops. The guys stand in tableau with their hands on their hips waiting for me to toss the ball back to them. I turn around to reach for it. I bend over and someone makes a sound as if I let one rip, and of course they all laugh. I toss the ball and chafe my way back to the lockers. It's almost time to go.

There's giggling coming from the locker room but that really isn't possible unless some of the boys are hitting puberty a little late or Beckett High is running a castrati program in the chorus. A piece of plaid fabric darts around the corner as I make my way down the aisle of lockers. Sticking out of mine and a few other lockers is a fluorescent orange flyer. I pull the flyer from the slats and unfold what I guess is a mistake. It's an invitation to a Halloween Party. An invitation! Now I'm sure it's a mistake since the party is at the home of Perry Parker, the Mighty Oak's henchman. No way would they want me around. Still.

I hold the paper in my hands. If they knew it was my locker, would they have slipped this in? If they knew it was the fattest boy at school, would they want me at their party? They probably didn't think I would be anywhere near the gym and this row of lockers is most definitely famous. Those invites didn't get here by chance, and the odds of me getting one is not even one in a zillion. It is Halloween though. I could – no, who am I kidding?

I can hear The Fart blow his whistle, signaling the gathering of the mindless. After he gives them his pep talk the guys will charge the locker room. For me, the trick to being in here alone is to get dressed fast and get out of the gym even faster. I'm distracted though, by the folded bright orange invitations sticking out of the other lockers. For one minute I think about taking each and every one and tossing them into the garbage. They would never even know there was a party. Instead, I fold up the flyer that is undeniably not meant for me, stuff it deep into my pocket and pull my shirt over my head. I slip on my sneakers, pull the velcro tight and flip the lights off as I leave. I always flip the lights off. It annoys the hell out of them.

***

Ten thirty in the morning is when I'm slated for lunch. In my book it's brunch. By the time noon rolls around, I'm *starving*. The cafeteria doors open and noises spill into the hall with the promise of a party, a daily party with open invites for everyone except me. You'd think I'd be used to it by now.

I drift past the Jockstraps, making sure to look down at my own feet, avoiding the obstacle course of sneakers trying to trip me up. Candy Sapperstein and her crowd share a pack of gum – their idea of a nutritious, gumalicious lunch. A few of the science geeks reluctantly wave. Collectively, my fellow science geeks and I are the Einsteins, champions of the Tri-State Area Einstein Challenge, the smartest game in the world of high schools. It carries about the same panache as being a contestant on Jeopardy, only no money. I nod at Enid, and walk toward the loser's table. They don't bother to make room for me. Acne covered faces, braces and nonentities squirm to fill the spaces next to them.

Instead, I head over to the window, pull up a chair, balance my lunch sack on my knee and take out two big sandwiches. From the window I watch Security check on the locks outside and someone making an attempt at fixing the hole in the fence. It's futile, the hole will be back tomorrow.

I look around the room to see if anyone else is holding an orange flyer, but I don't see any. If I got the invite legally, which technically I did, then I would legit be invited. But if I showed up at the party, would they laugh and turn me away at the door? The flyer starts to burn a hole in my pocket. I can feel it through my jeans, through a few pounds of flesh, taking on a life of its own. I can hear it talking to me, telling me there's no way I can go to a party filled with people who don't care about me. And even though I know that, I really want to go, but who am I kidding?

I slug down a Pepsi, crumple up my lunch bag and toss it in the trash.

The rest of the day is pretty uneventful except for me not being able to keep my mind on classes. Instead my mind is on Dylan. I start to write a list of the pros and cons of having him come to live with us.

Pros:

He could go to the Halloween party

That's as far as I get.

***

Saturday morning I don't get to sleep in – it's *Operation Dylan's Room.*

There are bags of garbage and my verging-on-broken desk chair in a pile at the base of the stairs. I step over an old comforter and push aside a stuffed animal, some mascot I have absolutely no idea what team it belongs to and why it wound up in my room in the first place. Not like I'm sporty or anything. I kick it toward the front door.

"Hello?" I yell up the stairs.

"C'mon up!" Mom calls. "We're fixing up your old room for Dilly."

I rarely go upstairs unless I really need to talk to Dad and he's in the shower or something. The stairs are old and steep, not like the ones to the basement. I'm afraid to use the banister, afraid I might break it. Leaning forward I take one step at a time until I'm standing in the doorway of my old room, slightly in need of oxygen.

"You're just in time." Mom wipes her forehead with the back of her hand.

The room is half empty – or it could be half full depending on how you look at it. For me, it could go either way. I pretty much moved everything downstairs that I needed and left the boyhood stuff behind. The bed is stripped and the empty bookcase waits to be filled with someone else's personality.

Mom pushes a box my way. "Where do you want all these memories?"

"Memories?" I have no memories. No party favors, no trophies, nothing really. What Mom refers to as memories is a box full of my comic book collection from the sixth grade and a handful of drawings I did out of boredom. I pick up one of the drawings and think maybe I'll take up art. It was a drawing of a Christmas elf from a *Draw! Go to Art School* brochure. I did copy it pretty well, though. Nah, who am I kidding?

I look out the window where I used to sit and watch the high school kids on the athletic field. Never did like it up here. "I'll take these," I say, dumping a stack of paperbacks into the box at Mom's feet.

Mom turns to the wall, puts her hands on her knees and takes a deep breath. When she turns around I can see she's trying to pretend everything is all right. I know Aunt Diane's death is killing her but she won't show it. Probably feels she has to be the strong one. Truth is, even Dad seems a bit nervous lately. He hasn't complained about one shipment in days.

"You think Dilly will like it here?" Mom asks, looking around the room.

"I think he will if you stop calling him Dilly, Mom." I let out an intentional snort, hitch my pants up and take the box from her. "I'll take this to my room."

Downstairs, I fix myself a snack and go to my TV spot on the couch. I unfold the list I wrote earlier – the list with the one thing about Dylan coming to stay. I think about more reasons why Dylan would be a good addition to our family. For one thing, Mom could stop nudging me all the time and annoy someone else. Dad could have someone to talk sports with. Me, I could maybe have a friend, even though he's my cousin, but more than anything he would be *obligated* to hang with me, whether he likes it or not. I hate to admit it, but I'm hoping he doesn't mind.

FAT_vs_FICTION@BLOGSLOP.COM

Photos of me: 0

Profile: Round

Friends: 0

PAST BLOGS:

Fat vs. Fiction

Meaty Fingers

French Fries
in Paradise

Judging the
Outer Shell

Who Wants
Seconds?

Guilt

Lean & Mean

*Click here
for more...*

Hog it, Blog it...

Today I overheard my mother talking to Miss Rubens about journaling everything she eats. Every morsel that touches her lips, she journals. She says if she writes everything down, she loses weight. If she forgets to journal, she gains weight. Then, Miss Rubens gives my mother a whole host of "cute quips" from her Weight Watcher's leader.

If you bite it, write it; If you drink it, ink it; If you nibble it, scribble it; and if you hog it, log it. So, I thought I would write down everything I ate from the moment I woke up till now. Here's what I've got so far:

2 bacon, egg and cheese croissant sandwiches
1 quart of chocolate milk
3 cream chocolate donuts
1 candy bar
2 cans of Dr. Pepper
1 bag of chips
2 peanut butter, banana and fluff sandwiches
another candy bar
1 triple decker ham, roast beef and cheese sandwich
another bag of chips
2 cans of Pepsi
Dinner would have been better but my parents had a real estate seminar to attend, so I ordered a large pepperoni pizza with extra cheese and a side of breadsticks (we know the guys that own the place so I get the breadsticks for free). Did I mention I ate the whole pizza?

Note to self: must try and eat something green. NOT!

Let's examine this. I wrote everything down just like Miss Rubens said she does and I don't think I lost any weight. Looking over my list of culinary items, I must say it was a lean day for me.

I think I'll go have a snack.

1 comment

Gross! You're such a Loserrrr!

28

Chapter 3

Usually I dread the walk to the library. It's the actual walking, not the destination, but today my mind is on something else. For one thing there's a movie-size Nestle's Crunch Bar in my pocket, waiting to have its wrapper peeled like a banana and devoured by yours truly. The other is the cousin thing. Mom is getting ready to close up my Aunt's apartment in Detroit. There's no funeral so she's bringing my Aunt's ashes and my cousin Dylan here, to Merryweather, New Jersey, where lately, the weather is anything but merry.

The possibilities creep in again. I could be *this* close to going to a party with cool people, not like the gaggle of geeks I'm about to hang out with. Up until now I've been an outcast. I'm a walking paradox, really – stuck in a world where everyone wants supersized everything, except for supersized people. Not like I'm the only one. It's not like I invented XXXL clothing sizes. I mean, think about supply and demand.

Then I think, maybe, just maybe, my luck is about to change. Maybe I won't have to hang out with people like the Einsteins. Who am I kidding? I'll never leave the Einsteins. I'm good at this. Truth is, they're the only friends I've got if you call a study group, friends.

I'm so preoccupied I walk into the crosswalk without looking and nearly get sideswiped by a woman on a bike. "Sorry!" I yell as she swerves, pedals away while flipping me the bird.

The library is almost as old as Beckett High and I think they shared the same architorture committee. I can see what they were trying to accomplish. They wanted Beckett and the other official buildings to have this Ivy League feeling of importance, but truth is, there are so many colonial structures in our town that this group of buildings is just out of sync with the rest.

"Where have you been?" Enid says in a loud whisper.

"Hello to you, too," I smile, taking the only empty chair left at the table while everyone waits for an answer to her question.

"At least we're all here now," Enid whispers.

"All four of us, *the smart quad*." I snort. This is the group I can pretty much be myself with, the smart self. I wonder why we're all not really friends in the sense of hanging out other than these genius gatherings. Maybe this is as good as it gets? Each one of us a unique geek.

There's Enid, our fearless leader who is great at organizing these study sessions. She actually has the potential of being one of *them*, instead of one of us, because she's really pretty. Not the kind of pretty Candy and those girls have to work at. Enid is just naturally pretty, but pretty and smart don't quite make it in Candy's world, so Enid's out. It's just as well. Next to me I think Enid is the smartest kid at school.

She pulls her thick blond hair into a twist and pushes a pencil through it to make it stay. It's the little things like that which make me think she really could be one of them. But then she pushes her seventies style, aviator tinted glasses up onto the bridge of her nose and talks with her usual formalities. "Let's continue, shall we?" When Enid speaks it's like the whole English department lives inside her mouth.

"Okay, what are we up to?" I ask, checking out Enid's boobs. I'm trying hard not to look but I think this is the first time I even notice she has them. It's like they just *popped*! Think of something else, think of something else – broccoli! No that will never work. Smothered in cheese it's not so bad. Liver. I hate liver, except when they're little pieces wrapped in bacon. Oh it's no use. I look down at my notebook and raise my eyes ever so slightly so I can look at Enid's boobs some more.

Enid pouts. "You know this is important to us, Rick. Important to Beckett!"

I look up at Enid and chase away my R-rated brain clot. It's not like her to act like the damsel in distress, pushing out her lower lip like that. Next thing I know she'll be batting her eyelashes at me.

"We need to come in first in the competition," Enid pounds her fist lightly on the table. "It is imperative that you show up in a timely fashion for these practices."

Now *that's* the Enid I know. Must have been a momentary lapse in identity. I'm feeling about two ounces of guilt but not enough to give into it. "So, where are we?"

"The challenge will be here before you know it," Kyle chimes in. He takes a deep breath and states his question like he's on the panel of some huge presidential debate. "Okay, if two typists can type two pages in two minutes, how many typists will it take to type eighteen pages in six minutes?" Kyle searches our faces for an answer. "Anyone?"

"Where'd you get this crap? I know we try to challenge each other but what's with the typist question?" Kyle is always trying to trump smarts and I always let him fail.

"Mensa." Enid defends Kyle's choice of question. "Do you even have an answer?"

It takes me no time at all. "The answer is six. One typist types one page in two minutes."

"Okay, okay," Kyle stammers. "I have another one that will definitely stump you."

Kyle is the third smartest in the group and even more of an outcast at school than I am. That's because Kyle is one of three openly gay students. He doesn't hide it, but doesn't flaunt it either. I am always amazed at the way he stands up for himself when it comes to the Jockstraps. Me, I just don't have the energy to stand up to anyone, but Kyle, he's not afraid of anything. I once asked him how he does it and he said once you come out to your parents, the rest is cake. The word cake is stuck in my head now and triggers a stomach growl.

"Go ahead, try me," I challenge.

"I thought you were straight?" Kyle laughs.

"Funny." I wiggle my fingers at him. "Let's go flamboyant one, ask a question."

"What about this, what about this." Kyle also says things twice. I think it's nerves or something. "If you count from one to one hundred, how many sevens will you pass on the way?"

"Oh, I know this one!" Enid jumps up from her seat and practically all eyes in the library are on her. "This one is not so obvious, as you would think it is, but it's soooooooo deliciously obvious!" She giggles with a signature snort.

"Go on." I have the answer but I let Enid get this one.

"Okay, so the obvious thing would be to say eleven. Right? But actually, it's twenty because most people forget the sevens in all the seventy numbers, like seventy one, seventy two... get it?"

Enid is pretty pleased with herself and to tell the truth, I'm pretty pleased with Enid. I think that maybe if I were tall and good looking, and didn't have acne, and could fit in a pair of jeans that weren't purchased at the fat boy's club, she might just like me in the way that boys and girls are supposed to like each other. Instead she's got Kyle as her best "boy" friend, and Max and I are just teammates.

"You're brilliant, brilliant!" Kyle pats her on the shoulder. "Okay Wunderkind, your turn, your turn."

The Wunderkind is Max, a transplant from Germany. Max and his mother moved to the states from Dusseldorf. I love saying the word Dusseldorf. The story goes that Max's great grandfather was some famous cuckoo clock maker and they had millions up the whazoo, but Max and his mother were excommunicated from their family after some scandalous affair his mom had with a rival clockmaker's son – definitely Doctor Phil worthy. So, they came to our little town to start over. I never understood why anyone would want to settle here instead of Los Angeles or New York or some other famous city. Max is fourth smartest in the group. His grasp of the English language freaked everyone out, even the teachers. Not one whole semester of ESOL and he mastered it.

"I have one," he says, straightening his tie. Max is also very formal. "Two men start at the same point. They walk in opposite directions for four meters, turn left and walk another three meters. What is the distance between them?"

"You know we don't use metrics," Enid scowls.

"Oh, come now, it's not hard for you." Max challenges Enid to a brain duel.

"Well, the obvious answer would be –"

"Fourteen!" I cut in. "But it's not, it's –"

Enid stares me down. "It's ten, Max. Ten meters because they make two right angles." Enid sits on chair, folds her hands in front of her and smiles. She's pretty proud of herself right about now.

That's the way it goes for the next two hours. We challenge each other till our brains feel like spaghetti, but the electricity we feel is mutual. Being smart isn't so bad when you can be smart around other smart people.

"Want to walk with me?" Enid asks.

"Sure," I say automatically. What else do I have to do?

I'm not the usual escort for walking Enid home, Kyle is. But, today, Kyle's mother is picking him up for psychological testing. She is convinced he's more than just Mensa and that he's a full blown genius. Of course we all think we're geniuses, but that's due to the fact we're smarter than most kids our age. And, yes, we are the Einsteins but we're not really in that galaxy of geniuses.

Enid and I walk in silence for the first block. I'm secretly glad she is taking it slow because keeping up with people is sometimes a real challenge. It's going to be so much easier when I can drive places.

"I'll be getting my driver's license soon and then I can drive you home. I mean, if you want me to." It was just a matter of weeks now.

"All four blocks, gee," she teases.

"It's still a ride." I smile.

"Are you going to get your own car?" Enid picks at her sweater. The weather isn't quite cold enough for a coat yet, but it's getting there. Winter is definitely around the corner.

"No. I'll probably use one of my parent's cars if they let me. It's not like I need it to go to school, but if I want to go to the mall or something..."

As if I ever went to the mall. It was rare that I would put myself in the position of being where other kids from school might be. The movies were okay. It's dark at the movies, but where was I going to shop at the mall. *The Gap* doesn't have anything that fits me, I need the "Gape". *Abecrombie & Bitch* barely has room in the aisles for me to walk through. Except for *FYI* or *EA Games*, there's no point in it. Nah, except for the food court, the mall isn't really my thing but it sounded good when I said it to Enid.

"I have a cousin coming to live with us." I don't know what made me blurt that out – as if Enid would care. But I went on anyway. "He's coming from Detroit."

Enid stops, turns and gives me her full attention, making me feel as if she's genuinely interested. I stop my eyes from wandering over her body and wonder if she likes me. I mean, *really* likes me, like the way boys and girls are supposed to like each other. My own conscience is telling me I'm an idiot, an inexperienced supreme dork, and I should get my brain back on the conversation track.

"What kind of fellow is he?" she asks.

Fellow? Sometimes Enid speaks as if she's stepped right out of a movie or something. Fellow, chap. "Enid, you're strange."

"How so?"

She was serious! "Enid, you say things like fellow, and chap –"

"I didn't say chap, I merely asked about your cousin." Enid pulls the pencil out of her hair and it falls around her face. She looks hot. "So, who is he?"

"He's Dylan," I answer. "His mom died, so he'll be living with us."

"Sorry for him. Do you mind that he'll be moving in?" she asks.

I don't think I mind it at all. The idea is growing on me. I kind of like the idea of having Dylan around. I'm just not so sure where he'll end up. I mean, at first all he'll have is me, but once he makes friends –

"Do you?" Enid breaks through my thoughts. Her hand brushes mine and a rush of electricity goes straight to my neurons. Was it on purpose? I know it wasn't on purpose. Who am I kidding?

"Do I what?" I've forgotten the question.

"Mind, that he'll live with you?" Enid pushes her glasses up higher on her nose. She has a sensitivity to light which is why she's always wearing those crazy aviators.

"Not at all." I look at Enid and notice my reflection filling her lenses. "It might be nice."

"Nice." She shakes her head in agreement. "I'm an only child. It is nice to have someone around once in a while, don't you think?"

I'm thinking about something else. "Are you going to the Halloween party?"

"Why would I want to go to *that* party? I wouldn't go unless I was *forced* to go. How about you?"

"Forced? Why would anyone be forced to go to a party?" Crazy thought.

"Were you invited to the party, Rick?" Enid's brows rose above her glasses.

"Sort of, I think. I mean, I have an invitation."

"Wow. I didn't think you even liked those people." Enid stops in front of her house.

I think she meant to say that those people don't even like me.

"I don't. Not yet, anyway. I'm thinking about going. I mean, I'm not sure I'm not going." God, I sound like an absolute moron.

"Well, here I am. Thanks for walking me. We can do this again sometime." Enid starts walking away and screams over her shoulder, "Don't forget to study. We have another practice next week."

I tap my head to let her know I won't forget and watch Enid walk up the driveway to her house and disappear inside. She once confessed she was scared of the dark among other things. I start to think about the things I'm scared of, and one of those things is if the invite was meant for me or not. I mean, it's not like everyone got one, but I did. I did get one.

FAT_vs_FICTION@BLOGSLOP.COM

Photos of me: 0

Profile: Round

Friends: 4

PAST BLOGS:

Fat vs. Fiction

Meaty Fingers

French Fries
in Paradise

Judging the
Outer Shell

Who Wants
Seconds?

Guilt

Lean & Mean

Hog it, Blog it

*Click here
for more...*

How come in movies, the fat guy is always funny

Think about it. Every time you see a fat guy in a movie, he's the comic relief, while the good looking model guy gets the girl?

I gave this some deep thought and came up with some answers...

For one, we'd make a terrible spy! It's not like we can run fast, leap over fences, or even get in a car smoothly. Ever watch a James Bond movie? That dude can leap from a building, grab onto a helicopter with one hand and then get dropped directly into his fancy sports car, driving away as if nothing happened.

Now, put us in that situation. We would leap off a building and plunge to our death in nanoseconds. There is just no way we'd survive or be able to grab onto any flying object in midair. Okay, say we're lucky enough to grab the tail of a helicopter ... it goes down. And being dropped into the seats of a fancy sports car? Four flats and a fat boy is all you're left with. Nope, won't work. I guess we're not cut out to be spies or action heroes.

What about doctor shows? Ever know one to have a really fat doctor? Sends the wrong message, like, "Oh, you won't die of a heart attack...look at me". Then the guy goes and dies of a heart attack anyway. Or worse! The doctor dies of a heart attack while trying to save someone's life 'cause he's so fat.

Cop shows are different. It's more common to see a fat detective or cop with an obligatory donut stuffed in his mouth. And you know that's no skinny latte he's got to wash down that donut.

I mean, the only time there's any attention paid to a fat person on TV is when they're trying to lose weight, like The Biggest Loser. What about The Biggest Winner? What if we won a hot dog eating competition? What if we competed in burping contests and could win 'cause we hold a heck of a lot more air? What if TV was only fat people?

72 comments

Right on dude. Let's start our own TV station and only have fat actors. It's about time we fat boys get the girl.

Chapter 4

Mom fidgets with her coat buttons, pulls down the visor and fixes her lipstick. "Now listen you two, no parties while I'm gone." She's still trying to put up a big front, like everything is A-okay.

I snort. Dad lets out a sigh. "It will be good for us," he says. "We'll bond. Yeah, that's it, we'll bond, right?" He looks at me and winks in the rearview mirror. I crack a weak smile.

"Bond." I try to put a little enthusiasm in my voice. "You and me, pizza and *beers*."

Mom doesn't get it. "No drinking. You're not old enough to drink." She hits Dad on the shoulder.

"I'm old enough," he kids.

"I'm not talking about *you*." She smiles at me and turns her attention back to the road.

"Yeah, like I'm such a big party boy," I say.

Mom clucks her tongue. "Maybe Dylan likes to be

social."

Dad drives slower than a baby sea turtle trying to find its way into the ocean. If there's a truck or slow car, you can be sure we're behind it. I shift my position, hoping by osmosis Dad will get the hint and change lanes.

"Maybe Dylan is a giant turd," I say under my breath.

"I heard that," Dad barks. "Remember our conversation?"

"Yes, Dad." I roll my eyes. I'm still not clear on why Dylan is coming to live with us and not some other family member. I mean, doesn't he have a dad somewhere? Every time I ask Mom, she skirts the issue and Dad simply won't fess up.

"What conversation?" Mom looks from Dad to me. Blue lights from the airport runways light up the night and our path to the departure drop off area. Mom doesn't wait for an answer and starts rattling off her directions and ingredients for a perfect male bonding weekend, *a la* Martha Stewart.

"The laundry is done and…"

"Honey, you'll be gone for two days, three tops!" Dad tries to get her to ease up but she doesn't hear him.

"…there's lasagna in the freezer that you can nuke, and don't forget the cold cuts. Oh, there's lots of those…and don't worry about me. As soon as they prepare Diane's body…"

Mom chokes on my Aunt's name. She takes a tissue and dabs at her eyes, then her nose and takes a deep breath.

"… Dilly and I will be on the first plane out. I hope Dilly has all his boxes packed … the movers are coming to get them tomorrow." Mom checks her face in the mirror. "Make sure everything is ready when we come home. I want it to be a smooth transition for Dilly."

"You gotta stop calling him Dilly," I insist. The kid is almost seventeen. "You do it to me, too. I don't want to be Ricky anymore. Rick will do fine."

Mom looks disappointed. "Rick? But we always call you *Ricky*." She says this like she's talking to a baby. Dad pops the trunk comes around to open her door.

"New dawn, Mom. Call me Rick." I smile and pull myself up to give her a peck on the cheek. "Have a nice flight."

Dad pulls the handle up and sets the luggage by her feet. I watch as they give each other a hug. To look at them, you would think they were the perfect couple. Both tall and graceful, both well dressed and immaculately groomed. I'm definitely adopted. Mom is still wearing her realtor badge. I think about telling her, but why bother. She wears her identity on the outside anyway. Dad gives her one more hug and she heads through the doors.

"Well, it's you and me, son." Dad buckles his seatbelt and we're off to a few days of male bondage.

***

We head over to the video store and rent horror movies. Mom doesn't like them and Dad thinks this is the perfect opportunity for a stag night.

"What do you think of these?"

I rummage through the pile of DVDs he hands me. *Killer Clowns from Outer Space, Eraserhead, Dressed To Kill?* My dad has officially lost it.

"They're some of my favorites. Wait till you see the one by David Lynch." Dad grabs a full size bucket with microwaveable popcorn, three chocolate bars and a pack of licorice twists.

"How about something current?" I pick up a DVD that has a guy with needles sticking out of his face. "Looks pretty gruesome."

"Aw, come on, I promise you're going to love these." Dad's grin toys with my sensitive wimp side. He grabs the DVD from my hand and puts it back on the shelf. "Please?"

Hell, I can't say no to the guy. He looks like a kid who just got away from his mom in the supermarket, grabbing everything that could possibly make him happy.

"Okay, let's go make some popcorn." I hand Dad the movies and walk away while he pays. I don't want the girl at the cash register to think all those candy bars and other crap is for me.

At home, I nuke the popcorn and convince Dad that the best place to watch movies will be downstairs in my bunker. We settle in for a night of madness and the first movie comes alive. Killer clowns with pointy, sharp teeth are taking over the universe. It's seriously whack.

"Wait till you see this... oh, watch this part... check out this clown!" Dad keeps a running commentary, proud of the fact that he can still remember every scene. "They're gonna turn these humans into cotton candy!"

Movie number two slides into the DVD holder and no sooner do the credits roll when I hear a light snore. Dad's fast asleep. I don't have the heart to wake him but I do have the heart to turn off another of his insane movie picks.

It's two a.m. when I flip the channels and land on an infomercial where some actress can show me how to have a younger, defined face, all with one mineral-rich color palette. Don't need it. I switch channels to yet another infomercial. Did you know that you can buy real estate with no money down? Honest. You can make millions! Channel up. This time they're showing before and after photos of a woman who lost over one hundred pounds.

"How'd you do it?" I ask.

"Diet, exercise and this handy weight loss pill, *Diminish*." She smiles at me. I look over at Dad. Did the television just talk to me? Dad's still sleeping. I pinch myself to make sure I'm still awake.

A woman's voice whispers through the television. "I'm talking to you."

I point my thumb at my chest. "Me?" I whisper.

"Uh huh, you." Her silky voice pulls me in.

I know this can't really be happening. I know that a television is just feed but still I'm glued, intrigued by the one yellow pill she is now holding between her thumb and forefinger.

"This little pill," she holds it out to me, "will change your life."

Change my life? I take the pill from her hand. She pushes a glass of water my way and tells me to drink. I tilt my head back and feel the pill slide down my throat. I look at the television and she's gone. Pinching myself harder this time, I make sure I'm not dreaming. Did I really just take a pill?

I walk into my room and stand in front of my mirror. My face looks the same but somehow more manly, more sculpted. My hair takes on a style, eliminating the cowlicks which keep me from ever looking neat, and slowly I see myself morph into a thinner, taller me. My flesh slowly forms into muscle, my stomach a perfect six pack. Heck, I look good. "Just one pill…" I hear her voice. "That's all it takes to change your life."

There's a tugging at my arm as flabby flesh morphs back where moments ago there was muscle. The tugging continues until I open my eyes and see Dad.

"You were dreaming," he scratches his head. "I didn't know you talk in your sleep."

A dream, that's all it was? One pill to change my life. Yeah right, who am I kidding?

"Go to bed. We'll watch the other movies tomorrow night." Dad salutes me and trudges up the stairs.

One pill. God I wish that dream was real.

I'm wide awake now. Sometimes all I need is a power nap and I'm up. My computer glows in the corner and I get an idea to browse weight loss pills, specifically "one pill weight loss." I don't find one, but what I do find is urban legend.

This girl got a diet pill from a magazine. The ad said one pill could cure obesity. She took the pill and within a week started to lose weight. The thing of it was, while she was losing all this weight she was famished, couldn't stop eating!

She ate and ate and ate but kept losing weight. One morning she wakes up with a bloody nose and a long flat worm lying next to her. Want to know what the scam of the weight loss pill was? Larvae. Yup, worm hatchlings, *tapeworm* to be exact. So, you take one pill and a worm lives inside your intestines eating up everything you put in your body. Somehow I didn't get it. I mean, if the worm is eating all the food, why isn't the worm getting fat?

I read more about tapeworms, becoming an expert. It was like that with most things. I had a head filled with useless information. Besides, you never know if a tapeworm question might come up in with the Einsteins. Anyway, it's hard to get rid of tapeworms. One post said the victim had to starve for a few days, getting the worm really hungry. Then they put warm milk next to the patient's butthole and the worm, hungry for the milk, comes out to see what the deal is. They trick the worm by moving the bowl further and further away until the worm is all the way out and then someone has to bash it over the head with a hammer. Ack!

So much for the one pill wonder.

All this info on dieting just makes me hungry. I take the stairs two at a time, catch my breath and head for the kitchen where I pour myself a big bowl of cereal. It will be morning soon. Maybe I'll just pull an all-nighter and watch some more

TV until Dad wakes up and we can start our male bonding rituals all over again.

***

"You know," Dad says over a foot-long sub, "I wasn't always this confident".

"You weren't?" I say, hoping he's not going into lecture mode. I felt this great diatribe coming on about *when I was a young man...*

"In some ways I was a lot like you."

"Oh, sure." Somehow I can't envision my dad as a fatty and the school joke. I suck down a Dr. Pepper. I don't even like Dr. Pepper but the Cola dispenser seems to have the wrong flavor and by the time I noticed I didn't feel like getting up out of my seat and trucking across the sub shop.

"I had acne." Dad makes his statement and models his glowing face.

Where was this coming from, I wonder, and why are we having this conversation? Dad isn't the type to get all sentimental, except maybe about his favorite horror movies. I don't think I know much about his years before he met Mom.

"I know it's not the same," he continues, "but it sure as hell kept me from wanting to talk to girls. I bet you know what that's like."

"Huh?" I'm not going there. Girls. He wants to talk about girls. "Dad, I'm not dating anyone if that's what you're getting at. I don't even want to date anyone…at least not in my school."

I'm thinking he hasn't got a clue. Not a clue! Does he *know* I'm a social outcast? Hint, Dad. Do I ever have anyone over? Do you see me going to a lot of parties? Do you see me go anywhere other than studying with the Einsteins?

"Well, I went to this doctor and he pretty much took care of my acne problem, but I was still feeling, well, shy, I guess." Dad's face almost looks boyish when he says the word shy.

"I'm not shy Dad, I'm *fat*." I stuff the hero square into my mouth so he'll get the picture.

"Rick, yes, you have, well, weight issues, but maybe we, I mean you need to see a doctor. Maybe there's a pill, or some program we can get you on. I know it won't be easy, but…"

I think about that dream. *Diminish*. "Dad, stop! I don't want to talk about it, okay." I push the rest of my sandwich away and eye the pack of chocolate chip cookies on the table. "I got it under control. I'm going to start dieting soon." I knew this was a lie. I was always going to start dieting *soon*.

"Okay, I was only trying to help." Dad sits back, defeated, and takes a deep breath. "It's just that your mom and I both want the best for you. You know that Rick."

"I know, Dad. I got it covered."

We leave, but not before eating the chocolate chip cookies.

By the time the weekend is over, Dad and I have watched eight horror movies, consumed seven pizzas, two cartons of ice cream, a bunch of subs, several bags of chips and Mom's reheated lasagna. I come home from school and spend the day picking up the house while Dad goes to bring home Mom and my new playmate, *Dilly*.

FAT_vs_FICTION@BLOGSLOP.COM

Photos of me: 0

Profile: Round

Friends: 0

PAST BLOGS:

Fat vs. Fiction

Meaty Fingers

French Fries
in Paradise

Judging the
Outer Shell

Who Wants
Seconds?

Guilt

Lean & Mean

Hog it, Blog it

Funny

*Click here
for more...*

Are we sinners?

The Seven Deadly Sins are supposedly the uber-vices. They are Lust, Gluttony, Greed, Sloth, Wrath, Pride and Envy.

I'm guessing everybody has a few of these vices in their everday lives, but what about the fact that we fat people have at least six out of seven!

Okay, let's take it from the top.

Lust. hell, who doesn't lust after someone. I mean we're fat, not stupid! 'nuff said.

Glutton and **Greed** go hand-in-hand, don't you think? I mean, if we weren't so greedy with our food we wouldn't be gluts. Now, I know gluttony. I went to glutton school. Gluttony comes from the Latin word gluttire, meaning to gulp down or swallow, to over-indulge, to over eat or drink. Well, I'm here to say that Gluttony isn't entirely frowned upon. It depends where you're from. In some cultures, gluttony was a sign of status. Who do you think was doing all that eating? The rich guys, of course. They had all the food. And why was that? Because they were *greedy*!

Sloth. Well, we're definitely guilty of that, but that's because we can't move very fast and in some cases maybe not at all. Are we lazy? I don't think so. My mind is always running. Hey, do you think you can burn calories by just thinking a lot?

Wrath. I'm guessing we're all a bit angry. It's a vicious cycle, really. We eat because we're angry and then we're angry that we eat so much. Speaking for myself, I try not to be too hard on myself. I save that for the masses who hate our big fat asses.

Pride. I think we're clear on that one.

Envy. Well, duh.

So fellow bloggers, I guess we're sinners after all. We're going *down!*

104 comments

Say one Hail Mary for every pound and I think we're good.

53

Chapter 5

My cousin slides out of the car and *oh no* is all I can think. He's built like a god, even more so than the Mighty Oak. Rather than go and help with the bags, I back into the house before Dylan sees me, prolonging the inevitable.

"Man you're way huge!" he says, wide-eyed when he enters the house.

"Way to go on the sensitivity." I bite the inside of my cheek till it hurts.

"Sorry, but Dude, you're *really freakin' big*." Dylan plants a right hook on my shoulder.

"Okay, I get it!" I rub the area that will most definitely bruise by morning.

Dad stumbles in, holding a stack of boxes, followed by Mom and her purse. She sets it down on the row of packages yet to be opened and smiles. "Isn't this nice, our new family!"

"Nice," Dylan and I say in unison. I don't think at this very minute either of us is too pleased.

"Why don't you boys go look at Dilly's, I mean, Dylan's room and Dad will bring these up."

"Helen," Dad whines. "My back is killing me! Why didn't you send these with the movers?"

"Dylan *needs* these things. Those movers are so slow. You know how it is? They group us with other moves."

"I got it, Dad." I bend to pick up one of Dylan's boxes and it's heavy. Dylan, meanwhile, stacks two and carries them up the stairs like he's holding two pizza boxes.

I hear Dad start to bitch about all the unopened boxes in the foyer. "Don't you think if I could move boxes I would have moved these downstairs long ago? Do you even know what's in these boxes, Helen?" Dad's voice diminishes with every painful step I take.

"This is your room." I drop the box in the middle of the floor, nearly taking my toe off. Dylan kicks off his sneakers, stretches his arms almost to the ceiling and looks out the window. I raise my arms when he's not looking, only to see how tall he is. Tall.

"Can I ask you something?" I clear my throat, readying for the next question.

"Sure, spill it," Dylan says.

"Where's your father? I mean, nobody ever talks about him. Like, why aren't you living with him instead of us?" I wait for an answer. The room looks smaller somehow and part of me is not so glad he's taking it over.

"Don't want me here?" Dylan digs his hands deep into the wells of his pockets, raises a brow and looks me straight in the eye. It's the kind of look a kid gets after he drops his ice cream but doesn't quite have a grip on the situation just yet.

"No, sure, I mean, that has nothing to do with it. Just wondering, is all." I feel like a jerk. Maybe I should have waited something like sixty minutes or six days before asking dumb questions. The guy's mother just died. I feel like an ass.

"Oh, I don't know. Nobody ever talks to me about him either." Dylan smiles. "So I guess that makes us even." He pushes the blanket over and sits down on my old bed, testing the springs by bouncing to some imaginary song in his head. "Anyway, this will be fine. At least that's what your mom says. It's what my mom said before – "

Dylan's looking kind of misty-eyed, like I swear he's going to cry or something. I look away and he rebounds off the bed to the window. "Smokin'! There's a basketball court right outside my room!" There's not a sign of the emotion he so blatantly tried to hide a minute ago.

I decide to drop it. I never even bothered to ask Mom

about it and made a mental note to do so, and if she won't tell me, I'll get Dad to. "That's your school," I point out. "*Our* school."

Dylan pretends to dunk a basketball, rips open one of his boxes and pulls out a real one. "Wanna shoot some hoops?" Dylan pulls on his sneakers.

"You talking to me?" I can feel myself start to sweat.

"Yeah, you. See anyone else in the room?" Dylan pulls trophies, yearbooks and other paraphernalia out of the boxes and tosses them on the bookcase. "Nice room," he says. "Great view!" That's my cue to leave.

I pop my head back in his room. "If you want to see where I am, come on down the basement when you're done." I turn to walk away but stick my head in one more time. "If you want to."

"Sure, guy. I'll just get the situation under control and check in with you." He winks.

Downstairs Mom and Dad are having one of their "discussions". The one where they don't want me to hear anything so they stand real close to each other when they're talking. As soon as they see me, they stop.

"How's he doing?" Mom asks, that worried look on her face.

"He's fine. Likes the room."

Mom gives a weak smile.

Downstairs I realize Dylan is going to be one of *them*, one of the Jockstraps, and he's living in my house. I start to think about how horrible it will be when he has his friends over and they ignore me or worse, notice me.

***

"Rick, come on up, it's dinner time." Mom calls from upstairs.

I'm watching a six week transformation tailor-made for me. That's what the guy on the TV says. In six weeks I can look like the other guy with the perfectly formed abs and arms cut like Hercules. In only six weeks! I hoist myself off the couch reluctantly. What if I miss the secret. What if I *can* be that way in six weeks?

"I'll be right up," I yell back, pressing the record button on the remote.

It's fact-checking time. My computer comes alive as I speed read through the Six Week Miracle site and check the comments. Evidently, if someone had the secret to changing a body from fat to thin and fit in only six weeks, it would be on the lips of every household in the universe. Instead it goes into the blah, blah, blah of a healthy diet and exercise – so much for miracles. I give up on the six weeks and think about the six course meal I could be having about now.

"What, are we having company?" Dad asks, sitting down at the dining room table. Normally we sit at the kitchen table and sling food at each other.

"Well..." Mom tucks a curl behind her ear. "I thought since it's Dilly's, I mean Dylan's first night here we could do something special."

"That's nice, Aunt Helen, thank you. Mom would do the same thing." Dylan sits next to Dad, in my chair.

"Oh, Diane." Mom's voice trails off and heads to the kitchen.

"That's my chair *Dilly*," I say. I always sit on Dad's right. That's because he's a leftie and jabs me with his elbow when he cuts his meat.

"No prob, my man." Dylan stands up and points to Mom's chair. Dad shakes his head no and Dylan takes a seat on Dad's left.

Mom puts out a spread as if there were company. We have roast beast with mashed potatoes, gravy, string beans and some kind of mashed squash dish. It's like a holiday feast ala Chef Mark. She passes the meat to Dylan.

"Guests first," she smiles. "Tonight you can be our guest. Tomorrow we sign you up for school and you're just another member of the household." She pushes the potatoes his way. "Gravy, Dylan?"

I'm about to be sick. Her tone is sugar sweet, as if she's about to break out in song and it's driving me crazy. Dad shoots me a look. I guess it's obvious I'm peeved.

"I'll take the gravy," I say. I make a hole in the mound of potatoes and pour in the gravy, until it spills over the edges onto my plate and over the meat. I look at my plate heaped high with meat and potatoes and at Dylan's plate, which is equally en mass. How is it he can eat like me and be the way he is? I take a bite and am suddenly self-conscious in front of Dylan. I don't look up to see if he's staring at me, but I feel like he might be.

"I'm not hungry." I push the plate away.

Mom jumps up from her seat and puts a hand to my forehead. "Are you sick, honey?"

I move her hand away. "I'm not sick, just not hungry, that's all." Dylan, Dad and Mom are all staring at me. "Can I be excused?"

"But it's a special night, Ricky."

"Rick," I correct her.

"Rick," she smiles. "Let's make Dylan feel welcome."

I try not to look at Mom. "Dylan, no offense but you don't mind if I leave the table, do you?"

Dylan sits with a blank look on his face. It's obvious he doesn't know what to say. He looks at Mom, then at Dad. "Uh, no," is about all he can muster.

"Okay then." I take my plate to the kitchen, perch it up on the counter and take a few massive bites. I hear light conversation taking place and use the time to snarf down my dinner. I grab two ice cream sandwiches and head down to my lair.

***

"So this is where you hang out." Dylan stares at the ice cream wrappers and takes a seat at the other end of the couch. "Sweet."

"Yeah, Grandma Irene used to live down here. I took it over after she died." I stood up hoping he wouldn't notice the big scoop in the couch. "Want a tour?"

"Sure." Dylan looks around the room and takes in the stacks of boxes. "What are all these?"

"Those are Mom's addiction. She's addicted to shopping on the internet, on the television, and in catalogs. The thing is, she doesn't even open half the boxes that come to the house." I point to the *Wii* on top of the TV. "I got that using her credit card and she didn't even know she didn't order it!"

"You use it?" Dylan's eyes grew wide.

"The *Wii*? Evidently, not!" I pause for effect but Dylan doesn't get the joke. "I thought the *Wii Fit* would be great, but as soon as I made my little guy, you know, my *Wii Mii*? Well, it registered my BMI, the character blew up like a balloon! I mean what an insult. You pay for something and the game literally tells you you're obese. It's defeat before you've even be –"

"Dude, I was talking about the credit card. You *use* her card?" Dylan's eyes roamed over the walls lined with cartons.

"Well, not always, just on rare occasions." I push a few boxes aside. "She hasn't a clue."

"What does she buy?" Dylan asks. The conversation is so strained, so benign, I think about livening things up.

"Want to see the fattest man in the world?" I stand taller. "You think I'm big? Wait till you see this." I steer Dylan to my computer and search for this fat guy in Mexico. "Check this out. They say he weighs, like, five baby elephants!" If that's the case, I realize I weigh more than one baby elephant.

"Whoa, what the heck does that guy eat?" Dylan turns the monitor toward him. "I once read where this guy was so huge they had to bury him in a piano case."

I step away from the computer. "He must have been

huge."

"Dude, way you're going..." Dylan bit his lip. "Sorry, you're right, not much on the social side. At home I hang with a pretty tough crowd. I guess that's why my Mom wanted me to come and live with your family."

"We have some of those guys here, too." I lead Dylan back to the couch. "They stop at nothing to make an ass out of me, especially at school."

"Sorry," Dylan says.

I almost believe he *is* sorry. I scroll down and see the guy who was once twelve hundred pounds lost five hundred, totaling nearly two baby elephants, and was getting ready to go outside for the third time in something like a zillion years. I shut down and join Dylan back at the TV.

"Look." Dylan shifts on the couch and turns to look me straight in the eye. "Aw, forget it."

"Forget what?" I hate when people do that. The whole 'never mind'. How can you never mind when now you have to know what's up. Never mind is out of the question.

"Well, look, if you let me, maybe I can help you. I mean, I'm no trainer but I know some things. You got that field right behind your house. You got a track and hoops out back. You got a gym right under your nose and I love the stuff. Maybe I could make you love it, too."

"Let's not go overboard." I take this in. He would get me to be what? Healthy? Fit? Thin?

"I'm not saying you're gonna drop all that weight, not right away, but we could at least start something." Dylan puts his hand on my shoulder. "Dude, I *need* a plan. I need to know what I'm doing. I mean, I'm not grieving or anything. I did that for the last two years that Mom was sick. It's almost a relief that she's finally..."

"I wouldn't really know how that feels but I can imagine it's tough." Losing Mom was not an option in my thought process and I pushed the idea out just as quick as it entered my brain.

"Yeah, but I need a plan. A project!" Dylan's face lights up. "*You* can be my project!"

"Project, huh?" I let out a deep breath, like I'd been holding it in ever since he started talking.

"You have a goal, don't you?" Dylan looks me straight in the eyes again.

"Now you're sounding like my Dad." I push his hand off my shoulder. "Well, there's a party."

"Goal? Party? A party is not a goal." Dylan scratches his chin, which actually has a bit of a goatee. "I don't get it".

"I want to go to this party. I've never been to a party, I mean, not one without hats and tooters! I got this invite to a

Halloween party, but I know if I show up they'll either use me as a piñata, hang me up by my underwear in public, or something equally embarrassing."

"You have the invite, so what's wrong with that?"

"I got the invite by mistake, I think." I pull the orange flyer off the side table and hand it to Dylan. "It was in my locker...by accident."

"By accident?"

"It was in all the lockers in the boys' gym and I don't think they knew one of them was mine." I take the invite and fold it back up. "They wouldn't expect me to be there of all places."

"Well, accident or not, it's legit. You got it." Dylan smiles. "Let's figure this out. In the meantime, you got sneakers?"

"Of course I have sneakers. I live in sneakers." I snort.

"Put 'em on." Dylan stands up and stretches. "It will be good to walk off that dinner your Mom made." Dylan takes the stairs three at a time. "I'm going to get my ball!" he yells.

If I can find mine. I start breaking into a sweat and I haven't even put my sneakers on yet. First of all, I don't walk off anything and secondly, who is he kidding? Me, a project!

***

"We're going out," I say to my parents whose jaws drop at the thought of me going anywhere, especially at night.

"Look at our boys," Dad says beaming. He's pure corn.

"Be careful?" Mom doesn't know what to say and it sounds more like a question than a statement. Dad's still standing there still with that goofy smile on.

"Don't worry, Aunt Helen, I'll take good care of Rick. We're just gonna shoot some hoops."

"Hoops?" Dad and Mom look at each other. I like the feeling of seeing them squirm.

"Yeah, we're gonna shoot some *hoops*," I echo. The fact that I never shot a hoop in my life was not going to hold Dylan back.

We walk till we come to the hole in the fence and Dylan slips through easily while he has to yank back the links to get me in. "C'mon." He takes off running.

I think about running, really, I do, but when I start to push off with one foot, the other doesn't follow. I'm frozen. I think about gym, about how they used to make fun of me when I ran in middle school. I am thrown back to a time where nobody picked me for their team and I was usually the last one standing. They really should have done the old one potato, two potato or picked names out of a hat. It was obvious nobody would ever choose me and the gym teachers didn't give a shit. I think teachers are as bullying as the kids sometimes, they just don't know it 'cause they never put themselves in our shoes, and certainly never in mine.

"What are you waiting for?" Dylan yells into the night. "Nobody's here, c'mon, Project."

I speed walk instead and by the time I'm at the basketball court, I'm tired, winded and ready to sit down.

"Oh no you don't, Project. Let's go." Dylan tosses the ball right into my stomach and it bounces off with an *oomph*.

"Could you not call me *project*?" I scowl. He's going to kill me. One way or another I'm going to die out here. Maybe that's his plan. Maybe he wants the basement instead of my dumb old room.

"Okay, look, take this ball and just stand here. This is the free throw line." Dylan situates me facing the board. "Take this ball and just toss it in there."

Just toss it in there? I look at the ball, try to get a feel for it in my hands and pretend I'm one of them, one of the Jockstraps. I've watched them enough to know what they look like when they're doing it, just not how they're doing it. I palm the ball in both hands and push it into the air where it lands with a thud, quite a distance from the hoop. I'm definitely more the cerebral type.

Dylan is clapping and I don't know why. I didn't do anything. "Good start, good start. Okay, watch me." Dylan moves further back from where I'm standing and gracefully sinks the ball right through the net. "Watch, it's all in the wrist." He does it again.

I move my wrists, pretending there's a ball in my hand and toss it into the air.

"Almost," Dylan moves to the side of me and puts the ball down between his feet. "Here, copy me." He moves his arms upward and over.

I try to imitate Dylan, but even without the ball I feel awkward, defeated. "It's no use."

"Dude, do it." Dylan hands me the ball and I copy his movements and after about twenty-something shots, the ball sails in.

"See! My Project." Dylan grins, his shiny, white, perfect teeth reflecting in the moon's light. "There's hope for you yet!"

I'm in shock. I sank a ball into a basketball net. Nobody would believe it. Hell, nobody is all I have. We try to shoot a few more but I can't get it in no matter what I try. "Beginner's luck," I say.

"It'll happen again. Give it time." Dylan stands with his hands on his hips and scans the area. "Track," he says.

"No," I say.

"I was just thinking out loud, that's all. I love running track. It's the only thing besides football that I probably get right. Maybe I'll try out for the football team."

"Good luck with that. You're going to have to compete with the Mighty Oak and his posse," I warn. "Not only are they football studs but they have the track covered, too."

"Rick, I ain't scared of nobody. Got that?" Dylan kicks at the dirt. "Especially a nobody with a tree name. I'll cut him down! I'll break his limbs!" With that he bays at the moon like a wolf in one of Dad's horror movies.

FAT_vs_FICTION@BLOGSLOP.COM

I eat, therefore I am...

...fat. I don't buy into that whole eat to live, don't live to eat deal. I might do a little of both. Okay, I do a lot of both, but hear me out...food is indeed your friend.

Photos of me: 0

Profile: Round

Friends: 5

PAST BLOGS:

Meaty Fingers

French Fries in Paradise

Judging the Outer Shell

Who Wants Seconds?

Guilt

Lean & Mean

Hog it, Blog it

How come?

Sinners

Click here for more...

Food can't yell at you.

Food can't poke fun at you.

Food will never leave you.

Food is absolutely comforting.

Food is there for you whenever you go looking for it.

Food tastes good and most of the time, it tastes great.

Food doesn't get boring.

You can take food to a movie.

Let's face it, food makes me happy.

Now, I'm here to tell you that there are a bunch of angry fat people out there, giving us a bad rap. The media tells us that if you eat fast food every day for a bunch of years, you'll end up obese and then end up on Jerry Springer. Girls are sticking their fingers down their throats just so they can wear some name brand on their butts. The diet industry makes a killing on people who are overweight, and there's a bunch of shrinks talking about us.

Maybe we were born this way, or at least born with the genetic disorder of being fat.

I'm thinking there's another planet in our universe where everyone is obese and that's the norm. Then we wouldn't be subjected to the superficiality of being judged by what's on the outside. It's what's inside that counts...if you can see past the Twinkies and hamburgers, the ice cream, the sandwiches, the donuts and chips and soda and... you get the picture.

162 comments

The shuttle leaves in exactly ten seconds. Get on it.

Chapter 6

"Give me all your papers." She takes them from Dylan. "This has to be quick, I have a closing at nine." Mom is driving the full block to sign Dylan in at Beckett High.

Dylan and I walk to school. I wonder how long this will last, how long before he sees how the school works and transforms into one of *them*. He won't want anything to do with me.

"So, tell me about this party again?" Dylan stands a full twelve inches over me and ducks low lying branches along the way. I sail right under them. "Will there be any cute girls?" he asks.

"Girls? Only all of them." I consider for a moment that I could possibly be in the same room with a bunch of girls and I swear, my heart starts doing this *ba-dum, ba-dum* thing. "I've spent a lifetime hating these people, hating them for taking punches at me any chance they get."

"Punches? They hit you?" Dylan stops in his tracks, balling up his fists.

"Naw, not literal punches but I bet they would if they could! More like making fun of me, ridiculing me, a shove here and there."

"So, you really *like* these guys?" Dylan pokes me in the side. I try to push his hand away before his fingers sink into my flesh.

"Yeah, *loathe* them. Here's the gist of it, even though I want nothing to do with that crowd, the Jockstraps, the so-called 'beautiful people', I still wouldn't mind being part of a – I mean, I don't want to be a football star, that's not my M.O., but I do – oh, what's the point."

"There is a point." Dylan picks up the pace. "Like if you could be a fly on the wall and check out the party without them knowing you were there, so you could see how the other half lives?"

The guy gets me. Who knew!

"Costume," he says.

"No. No costume is going to hide what I've got going on here." I grab my big belly flesh to make a point. I'm thinking about all those fat football players on TV. They must get fat once they go pro, all that money, all the restaurants and take out you could want. I think about them with their meaty bellies hanging free. What's up with that? Have they no shame?

Costume. I could go as a pro football player, put black stuff under my eyes, borrow some shoulder pads, a helmet. Heck, who am I kidding?

"We'll think of something, my little Project." Dylan smiles.

"First of all, there's nothing *little* about me. Secondly, stop calling me *project!*" I poke Dylan the way he poked me earlier. "We've arrived." I stop short of the walkway leading to the school and let Dylan take in the panoramic view.

The city takes pride in the fact that Beckett High is the oldest building for miles around. Red brick hides behind ivy covered walls and later additions are evident by the mixing of styles – Georgian, Colonial, and then throw in some Ionic columns and you've got a mish mash of an eclectic and somewhat ominous building. It would be perfect in a Stephen King film or *Night of the Zombie Alumni*, if there were such a movie.

Speaking of movies, the cast of characters are all in place. The Mighty Oak and his crew lean against columns, guarding the front of the school. Oak's brow furrows as we near. He looks at Dylan and nods. Dylan nods back like it's some kind of secret language between gods. Why don't they teach that as a required language?

"That's the guy I was telling you about. He's the one that likes to make my life miserable every chance he gets." I avoid Oak's eyes.

"That's the tree guy? I could kick his ass, easy." Dylan puffs out his chest and stands taller. He checks out a junior in a skirt that is most definitely not fingertip, school-regulation length. "The school's pretty cliquey, huh?"

"That's putting it mildly. There are barriers, walls, invisible lines you dare not cross if you don't belong," I say this out of the corner of my mouth, just above a whisper.

"Which clique are you in?" Dylan turns his attention to a cluster of giggling girls.

"You're kidding, right?" I maneuver myself through the doors of the school. Lucky for me, both are open at the same time. "No clique. I'm a man without an island, or an island unto myself. Nobody lets me in." The hope I was feeling with Dylan peters out with every word. "C'mon, I'll take you to the office."

Ms. Hatchet, the typing teacher and office sentinel, sits at the front desk tightly nibbling on a pencil eraser. "What do you boys want?" she says with a dismissive, raspy voice.

I'm distracted by the new growth of hairs sprouting from her chin. "Evidently, someone didn't shave today," I whisper to Dylan.

"What's that?" Hatchet looks me straight in the eye.

I don't even know why I said that. I'm not generally mean spirited and I certainly don't like it when I'm the one being talked about. "Sorry," I say under my breath, even though I know she couldn't possibly have heard me.

"How's that?" She burns a hole through my head with her laser glare, her own eyes twitching maniacally.

"He's new." I push Dylan toward Ms. Hatchet. "I mean to say, has my Mom been here? Is she still here?"

Hatchet points with the pencil to the principal's office. "Go on."

Dylan walks straight back and puts his hand out to greet the principal. I watch his suave walk, his self-assured manner. I stand up straighter and try to suck in my gut. Who am I kidding?

"All set!" Dylan is holding his new schedule. "First class is English. Lead the way, my man."

I dump Dylan off at O'Leary's classroom. He's the best English teacher in the whole school. He'll cover the history of rock n roll for a whole semester and make it read like poetry.

"See you at lunch." Dylan disappears through the doorway.

Lunch. Oh, that will be rich.

***

In science, we're taking the cellular structure a step further. Lettuce leaves.

Hartman draws a Venn diagram on the board, his marker paused in mid air for the next notation. "Why did the lettuce leaf become stiff in cold water?"

"'Cause it was a horndog?" Someone says loud enough for the whole class to hear.

Hartman ignores the wave of giggling and moves onto the next question. "Alright then, which cells in the epidermis of the lettuce have chloroplast?" He waits about a full five seconds before looking directly at me. "Anyone?"

"That would be the guard cells," I answer as if on autopilot.

"Correct. The guard cells look like two sausages with the ends touching. They contain chloroplast." Hartman writes on the board and moves onto other cellular structures within a lettuce leaf.

Is it just my imagination or does he compare everything to food?

"Ewww," Candy pushes the microscope at me. "This is grosser than our cheek cells."

"*Your* cheek cells," I correct her.

She pops a new piece of gum in her mouth and leans closer. "Who's the guy you were with this morning?"

I pretend not to hear. Candy kicks me under the lab table. She leans in to whisper and I can smell the perfume of her shampoo rise to my nose. If I had to name it I think I would call it *Forest of Passion.* "Who was it?" she demands.

"Who? Oh, the big guy? That's my cousin. He lives with us now." I comb my fingers through my hair and pretend like it's no biggie, as if it were normal that I would have a cool, Adonis-like creature by my side on any given day.

"Your *cousin*?" She looks at me in wonder. *"As if!"*

"What's that supposed to mean?" I whisper louder this time. "I can't have a cousin?"

"Not *that* hot!" she says smugly, leaning back and folding her arms in false victory. "You must be adopted."

"I've often thought that I was." I whisper. Where were the genetics? Both my parents are tall and thin. All of Mom's side is tall and thin. We weren't that close to Dad's side but as far as I know, no fatties there.

"Well he *is* my cousin." I grab the microscope and peer at the cellular tissue, dissecting what I can with the toothpick in my hand. Dylan. It's just a matter of time before he gets the girl, too.

Candy follows me from science class into the cafeteria, and ditches me as soon as her friends notice I'm there. Dylan walks in with The Oak trailing alongside. Oak stops at the Jockstrap table and introduces my cousin. Lots of knuckle banging and nods ensue. Dylan takes a look around, spots me and walks over to my place at the window.

"Nice view." He sits on the window ledge, one leg dangling in an oh so cool way that I couldn't maneuver if I tried.

"Yeah, it's not home but it's mine." I lift my chin to point at the masses. "No room at the inn."

"I could fix that." Dylan smiles.

"No thanks. I'm good." I'm just about finished with sandwich numero uno. "Where's yours? Mom packed you one, didn't she?"

"Yeah, she did. I'll eat it later. I hate eating in lunchrooms – gives me the skeevies." Dylan crosses his arms and takes in the clusters. "I met the tree guy in my last class. Wants me to try out for the football team, says someone got hurt and there's an opening."

"I knew it," I say quietly.

"Knew what, bro? You think I wanna hang with *those* guys? I eat those guys for breakfast back in Detroit. That guy, he's a flamingo. Pretty to look at – all height and nothing else."

"The Mighty Oak doesn't think so." I snarf my second sandwich, crumple the bag and think about sailing it into the waste basket. I think again. If I miss, it will just be one more thing to pick on me for.

"Of course he doesn't. He's used to being the big man on campus. I'm here now." Dylan clears his throat, stands up and does that thing with his chest again, like a rooster seeking out a mate. It works, too! Candy Sapperstein magically appears in front of us, snapping her gum.

"Aren't you gonna introduce us?" she says, leaning on my shoulder like she's my best bud.

"Dylan, Candy." That's all the intros I can muster. I shake her off my shoulder and she gets all jittery.

Candy twists the ends of her hair between two fingers, blows a bubble and pops it before speaking. She runs her tongue across her bottom lip and then her top, pulling off the remnants of pink goo. "Rick tells me you're his cousin?"

"Is that a statement or a question?" He looks at me and talks like she's not even there. "I hate it when chicks talk like everything is a question. You know, how the words go up at the *ennnnnnd?*"

Candy is either in shock or too dumb to notice that he's

just insulted her. "So, are you?" she asks.

"Ah, it *is* a question then. Well, yeah, I'm Dylan, Rick's first cousin, mother's side." He smiles and I can almost see her shaking.

Dylan's got the same stuff The Oak does. If I can figure out what it is, I can bottle it and sell it to all the science and computer geeks of the world. Imagine, charismatic geekazoids suddenly showing up on the red carpet with gorgeous actresses and swimsuit models. Nothing left for the hot guys. I can dream, can't I?

Candy studies her shoes, letting her focus cross over to Dylan's shoes, up his legs and finally to his face. "I'm Candy."

"You already said that!" Dylan rolls his eyes.

"Oh, yeah, duh!" Candy giggles, shakes the words out of her head and looks back to her table of friends. "You wanna come make some new friends?"

"Maybe later, thanks. I got business here with my man Rick." Dylan nods his head a few times like he's got that song going again. "Maybe later." And like that, he dismisses her.

Candy looks like she doesn't know what to make of him and just stands in front of us with a blank expression. A whole minute goes by before she actually speaks. "Oh, okay. Welcome to Beckett."

"Yeah, thanks." Dylan waves her off and Candy fluffs

out her hair with her fingers, checking her reflection in the window before returning to her table. *What's this guy got? Better yet, can I get some of it, sell it on the House Beautiful Shopping Network?*

"That was Candy," I say.

"Yeah, I got that part. She got anything upstairs?" He points to his head.

"Plenty!" I point to his chest.

"You got that right!" Dylan and I have a good laugh. I can't remember ever laughing inside these walls.

"I'll catch you later." Dylan strolls through the lunchroom, meeting nobody's gaze. He almost coasts above the floor. I spy The Oak debating whether or not to get out of his seat and follow. He moves to, then decides no. I'm not sure, but I think that's worry written all over the Mighty Oak's face. As Dylan would say, *sweet*.

***

By the end of the school day, I've lost Dylan. I didn't see him in the hallways since lunch and now he's not even outside. I start the walk home and see The Oak and the jockstraps heading right toward me. I'm ready for them. Whatever it is they're going to do this time, I'm ready. I hold my breath as they near and *whoosh*, they're gone. Gone! I pick my head up and look around but they sail past me without a word. I don't want to stare at them but I don't know if Dylan is with them either.

I don't know what just happened, but I feel like I've escaped a major ordeal, like a meteor just missing planet earth, and my heart races from the expectation alone.

FAT_vs_FICTION@BLOGSLOP.COM

Photos of me: 0

Profile: Round

Friends: 5

PAST BLOGS:

Fat vs. Fiction

Meaty Fingers

French Fries
in Paradise

Judging the
Outer Shell

Who Wants
Seconds?

Guilt

Lean & Mean

Hog it, Blog it

How come?

Sinners

*Click here
for more...*

The art of find cuisine

You know when you're so hungry you could eat a bear? I'm hungry like that all the time. I'm perpetually hungry. Sometimes, it's like having 500 channels on satellite TV and not having anything to watch.

I'm that hungry but don't know what to eat...

I'm here to tell you about the art of FIND cuisine. It is indeed an art because you have to take random things that you find in your fridge and kitchen cabinets and try to come up with something that might just end your hunger...at least for a while.

Tonight I had to fend for myself 'cause the folks went to another real estate seminar. Usually we have a fridge full of prepared foods but I didn't want any of it. What I wanted was pasta with chicken and peanuts and a peanut butterish sauce, so I whipped up some tasty dish without really knowing how I did it. Get this...it was great!

You gotta think we're masters at taste. With the amount of food we eat, we should be able to come up with some brilliant ideas. Next time you're watching The Food Channel, notice how a lot of those cooks aren't so skinny. How can they be? Ever see them saute anything in cooking spray? Not likely. These guys are the real deal. THEY USE BUTTER! They don't just sprinkle on the salt, they pour it on! And they don't use skim milk, it's heavy cream for these pros.

I'd love to be a taste tester for one of those guys. I'd eat a whole bowl of stuff and be like, nah, this doesn't taste good, just so they'll make more and I can taste it again. Now that's a job we're worthy of!

Here's my take on it: If it's fat free, calorie free and sugar free, it's probably taste free. That's why anything that tastes really, really good is really, really bad for you.

Life just isn't fair. I'm hungry.

184 comments

Ever try Pepsi milk? It's amazing.

Chapter 7

The delivery guy is at our front door only he doesn't have any packages. This is most unusual.

"Hey," he says with about as much intelligence as a gnat.

"Hey?" If he doesn't have any packages, what is he doing here? "Got something for us?"

"Nah, your brother signed for them." He tips his brown cap and heads for his truck.

Brother? Dylan is home already? I push open the door and nearly trip on the new load of boxes in the foyer. Dylan pokes his head out of the kitchen. "Those all Aunt Helen's?"

"Probably." I study the labels on the boxes which are all made out to Mom. "Yeah, all hers." I walk into the kitchen where Dylan is fixing a large salad.

"I've been here what, one week, and I think there are

deliveries every single day. How much dough does she spend?"

"I'm thinking Mom's working her way to *nillionaire* status, as in nada, nil, no money, broke. She makes big money, they both do. Mom can turn a house around like nobody else. But, she doesn't even know what she has in these boxes! If there's a big sale, she has to buy it that very minute. If you listen to Dad, he's like, *'Helen, if you could be just a little less reactive, you might not buy so much.'*

"Aunt Helen would never make it as a nillionaire." Dylan spills dressing into a bowl. "Want some?" he asks.

I wince. The hairs on the back of my neck stand straight up. "Do I look like the salad type?"

"That's exactly why I'm asking, my Project." Dylan tilts the bowl so I can check out the ingredients. It's loaded with chopped veggies. He sprinkles in a handful of cut up turkey roll and roast beef. "This is loaded with protein. Keeps you full."

"Nothing keeps me full." I walk over to the fridge, grab the bread and get to work making my sandwiches. Dylan watches me pull out a bottle of Pepsi, drink the first third right from the bottle, pour the milk in and shake it up.

"Dude, that's disgusting!" Dylan backs away.

"How come all of a sudden it's disgusting? You haven't

said anything before." I take a big gulp.

"Timing. I was being polite for the first week. Now I'm, uh, comfortable here. I consider this place my crib."

"Crib. Nice." I'm feeling a tender moment coming on and steer the conversation away. I wipe my mouth with the back of my hand. "Dylan, remember Grandma Irene?"

"Not in the least. I know she lived with you guys, but..."

"Right. Well, Grandma Irene used to make egg creams, chocolate egg creams that were the atom bomb of beverages! But this really is amazingly good. Try it." I push the bottle toward Dylan and he pushes right back.

"There are some things in life that are just unnatural Dude, and that Pepsi thing with milk is one of them." He shivers.

"Suit yourself." I balance the plate of sandwiches in one hand and the bottle of Pepsi in the other. "Doctor Phil, downstairs, ten minutes."

Dylan follows me and we settle into our spaces, me in the fine ass dip of the couch and Dylan at the other end with his feet propped up on the boxes.

I can hear every chomp Dylan makes on his salad. It's distracting me from the really important stuff Dr. Phil is talking about. Here's this guy who's addicted to gambling, playing the horses, betting his entire earnings on football games. His house and family are in jeopardy.

"You're an idiot!" Dr. Phil yells. The crowd applauds. I down my last gulp of Pepsi milk and let out a belch that lasts just about a full fifteen seconds.

"Gross," Dylan swipes at the air and lets out a burp to rival mine. "C'mon, let's ditch Dr. Phil and hit the courts." Dylan is up and ready. "We'll play a little one-on-one."

"You're kidding, right? You know I'm no good at that." I whine. "Besides, my food isn't digested. I'll upchuck." I felt a little green just thinking about it. Since Dylan has come to live with us, I've spent more time on the athletic field than I have my entire high school career. The thing of it is, I don't give him too much of a hard time 'cause it's pointless, he'll get me out there one way or another.

"Okay cousin, you can watch me shoot some hoops. Let's go." Dylan runs up the stairs and out the door.

***

"He shoots! He scores!" Dylan yells as the ball sails through the air and dips right into the basket. "The party is coming up."

Don't think I didn't know that. I've secretly been counting the days. Now we've got exactly seven days till the party...lucky number seven...then again, there are seven fundamental types of catastrophes and this might just be one of them.

I've been thinking about the costume ordeal but Dylan has football tryouts on his mind. For a few days it was all about him getting settled and feeling part of the family. For me, my party dilemma went AWOL. But now that he's bringing it up, maybe we can brainstorm some ideas.

He stands in front of me and dribbles the ball. "Reason why you want to be anywhere near those guys, does it have to do with that Candy girl?" Dylan bounces the ball off the rim of the bracket again and again. "She's always hanging around the field, drives the guys crazy. She's got restless lip syndrome or something – never stops talking. Personally, I think she's a little attention starved."

"Nope. Not Candy. Not anyone really." Although, if Candy or one of her gum chewing pack of friends showed me the time of day, yeah, I could maybe be interested. "Dylan, I'm in high school and not once have I been asked to a cool party. I'm not like you – not like anybody, really. I just know if I could be at this party without anyone knowing, it would be near perfect." The smell of garlic or something drifts in the air and makes my stomach growl.

"I was thinking about that, thinking about the fly on

the wall thing. Dude, the whole point of a party is the social thing. You know, boy meets girl." Dylan tucks the basketball under his arm. "Smell that?"

"Smells good like Pizza, or Szechuan" Damn. I should've said *what smell*. I never like bringing up the subject of food, people might think that's all I think about, which of course is mostly true.

I stand to go. "Being a fly on the wall wouldn't be so bad. I could watch, you know, look at girls without them knowing."

"I think that's illegal, Dude!" Dylan laughs.

"Not creepy like that. Just to be in the same room as a bunch of girls who aren't mocking me, you know, with the looks they usually give. If I could sit or stand quietly in a corner..."

"So," Dylan taps his chin. "We need to find you a mask."

Not too bright this cousin of mine. "Uh, Dylan, I think I'll need more than a mask for camouflage. We've only got a week. What can we come up with in a week?"

Back at the house, Dylan is like a scavenger in the basement, sniffing out treasure. "Does Aunt Helen have any really big boxes, like wardrobe boxes or something?" Dylan looks around, cranes his head toward what was once my grandmother's kitchenette and spots the refrigerator box at the far end. "What's in that?"

"That is a box filled with tons of other boxes. Mom's idea of consolidation. Nothing makes sense in the maze of cardboard."

"*That* is your new costume." Dylan motions with both hands toward the big box like the host of a game show.

"I'm a box?" I'm confused, is what I am. Suddenly I'm the round peg in the square hole, if holes can be square. Square though, definitely my fit.

"No, it's what we're gonna do with the box." Dylan sits down on the couch and studies the box in the corner. He rips a piece of line paper out of a notebook and starts scribbling.

I've been dreaming up a costume, myself, that is, while I was dreaming up a way to go to the Halloween party. "I was thinking, maybe I could be a scary table. You know, how you cut a hole in a box, put my head through it and drape a table cloth around it so it looks like a scary chopped off head!" I love my idea. "We could drip blood out of my mouth, and — "

"Nah, they would know who you are, besides, I got a better idea." He folds up the paper, slips it into his back pocket and says nothing.

I wait to hear the details while flipping on my TiVo, but Dr. Phil is wrapping up his show and I forget about the costume for a while. The wife is crying and the good Doctor tells the guy that he needs to shape up, save his family, save for their future, save himself!

"Save yourself!" I yell at the screen.

"Oh, the drama!" Dylan pretends to cry and tosses a pillow at me.

"Yeah, I love this crap." And I do, too. "I used to watch all these shows with Grandma Irene when she lived down here." Maybe it's the whole getting lost in other people's celluloid lives that works for me. Better than getting lost in my own.

Dylan jumps off the couch with a gigantic, toothpaste commercial smile. "Okay, I got it," he says. Let's go to your computer and look up vending machines." Dylan rises off the couch and puts out a hand to help me up. I don't take it. I inch myself to the edge of the cushion and give one good push, trying to stifle any grunts.

"You want to buy a candy machine?" I don't know where he's going with this.

"No, Dude, I once saw something about human vending machines from Japan. Let's take a look and see if we can take that big box and turn you into a vending machine. I can go as a repair guy or something, you know, with my butt crack showing." Dylan starts searching and whammo, it really exists! "The problem is you can see the chick's face." Dylan looks me over head to toe. "We'll do it up a little different, this way nobody will know it's you inside and you get to watch the party, like a fly on the wall, just the way you said."

"Brilliant! You're actually smarter than you look." I hit Dylan on the back, nearly sending him crashing into my computer monitor.

Dylan straightens up. "Are you ready?"

"As I'll ever be. What do we need?" Mom took art classes at the Museum one year and there's every supply you can imagine, purchased of course on the *House Beautiful Shopping Network*.

"Paint? Some foil," Dylan scratches his head. "I dunno, we'll improvise as we go along. We start tomorrow."

"Cool." Suddenly I'm feeling uplifted, even though the thought of anyone or anything lifting me is comical at best. Some unfamiliar sense of elation seems to have crept in – I'll go with that.

***

For the next two days when we come home from school, Dylan and I work on the vending machine costume like the end result will be a naked woman, ready to smother us with kisses. I can dream, can't I? Okay, that's my fantasy, but Dylan is really focused. I keep reminding him that there's no real payoff, that I'm just going to try and blend into the woodwork and nobody will be the wiser.

"Dude, this is going to be a masterpiece! Everyone will want to know who's inside." Dylan works some foil around the fake knobs while I cover the box with metallic silver paint. "Pay no attention to the man behind the curtain!" He says it just like the *Wizard of Oz*.

"We're not going to tell them who is inside, right? This is supposed to be me, incognito." Paint splashes onto my white sneakers as I swirl the brush around the can. "The whole point of the costume is so I can hide out, remember?"

Dylan pulls at a roll of plastic wrap and plies it over the windows that will soon reveal my drawings of candy and soda. "I know, *buzzzzzzzzz*. Don't worry, we won't tell them till maybe the end."

"No, Dylan. No telling anyone, ever." I feel my face go all hot. If there was one thing I didn't want, it was for any of the kids at Beckett High to have the chance to ride me, even if it was a great costume.

"All right, take it easy." Dylan mumbles something under his breath but I don't catch it.

While we paint, mold, tape and staple my costume

together I realize I'm supposed to be somewhere else. I'm supposed to be at a picnic with the Einstein team. A picnic in the middle of October! Enid thought the fresh air would open our minds up, and what Enid says, the brain clan does. Well, the other two, anyway. All the brainy kids at school march to the same drum, except me. They hang out together, read books together, challenge each other to brainage duels – not for me. I generally prefer Dr. Phil and the world through a flat screen plasma TV. At least I did until Dylan came around. Anyway, it's not like I really *need* to study for the Einsteins. I just show up because I have to.

"Dylan," I put down my paintbrush. "Do you mind if I disappear for a while? I have something to do."

"Sure, Dude, just hand me that tape roll and a Coke and I'll be fine." Dylan goes back to pulling the plastic wrap so tight, if not for the reflection, you could barely tell it was there. "A masterpiece, I tell you."

I can still hear him humming as I leave the house.

FAT_vs_FICTION@BLOGSLOP.COM

Photos of me: 0

Profile: Round

Friends: 5

PAST BLOGS:

Fat vs. Fiction

Who Wants
Seconds?

Guilt

Lean & Mean

Hog it, Blog it

How come?

Sinners

Find

BBW

Whales

*Click here
for more...*

Big beautiful women

Okay, I admit it, I surf the web to see if there's any hope for love.

Looking for love took me to a website totally dedicated to matching big women with big men! No bull! It's a plus-size personals site for big beautiful singles looking for friends, romance and matrimonial bliss. Too bad I'm not old enough, but if I was...

There's a whole world of fat people out there seeking other fat people. Dating services, friend services, cultural gatherings for fat people only. Be amongst your own kind!

I'm here to tell you fat boys like me that we don't really want fat girls. No offense fat girls reading this blog, but why would we want to seek eternity with the likes of our own kind. I mean, don't you dream of being with a pageant queen? Don't you dream of having the same hot chicks that all the other guys get. Just because we're fat teens, doesn't mean we want fat beauty queens. I'm not discriminating, just being honest here.

On further investigation, there are actually people out there called chubby chasers. Girls, hide your eyes. Guys, this is not a chubby in the sense that you know (LOL). Okay, girls, you can open 'em. There are real people who are thin that seek hefty people like us. I just don't see it.

I don't think we're destined to spend our lives alone, but if we keep going the way we're going, we might not have a chance.

Diet.

Tomorrow. That's the best day of the week to start.

Tomorrow.

227 comments

Love doesn't discriminate, you ass! Fat girls rule.

95

Chapter 8

It's all about Enid and some whack idea about fresh air and the fall weather. Her theory: our minds will be that much sharper surrounded by nature, like a think tank retreat. Kyle and Max are already in the park prepping away for our meet.

"Crazy idea, Enid." I grab an end of the blanket and pull it tight to one side. "It's autumn, and you have us at a picnic." Actually, I never thought I would be on a picnic with anyone other than my family, and come to think of it, I've never been on a picnic with my family either. Mom is dangerously allergic to bees and Dad, well, Dad isn't exactly nature guy, and we all know about me. But here I am sitting on a blanket, under a tree with Enid and my fellow brain gang gearing up for the big competition. I wonder if Einstein liked picnics. I do know that he felt very strongly that all of nature must be described by a single theory. At least that's what he said in his Nobel lecture in 1923. Maybe that question will come up today.

I'm partially aware of the conversation taking place as I watch Enid set four paper plates in front of us, unwrap four sandwiches, break apart a big bag of chips and pass a bottle of water to each of us.

"Hey, Enid, your glasses, they're different." Brilliant. I'm a real genius with that opener. Her glasses tint even darker as the sun hits them. I never noticed they did that before. They always have the slightest lavender tint and now they're a dark, stormy purple.

"Polarization. You're aware I have very sensitive eyes. Sunlight is exceptionally difficult." She smoothes out the center of the blanket and drops a little bag of cookies in the center. I could eat that whole bag in one big bite, but I don't. I barely touch my sandwich and chips. As long as my stomach doesn't do the thunder routine, I'm fine.

With lunch out of the way, Enid pulls her hair into the obligatory twist on top of her head and sticks a pencil through it to hold it in place. I like her hair down. I thank the gods that she's wearing an oversized sweater which completely hides the fact that she's got boobs, which completely gives me no distractions.

"Let's walk a little. We can think better after all that eating." She stands, stretches and puts a hand out to Kyle, whose skinny little body nearly floats when she helps him up. Max grabs the cookies and follows. I turn over onto my knees and push myself off the blanket and stand upright as if mimicking the chart of Neanderthal to present day man. What was she thinking having a picnic on the ground, and now walking? She's killing me.

"You first," Enid directs. "You keep asking questions until you stump someone. Then they take over."

I'm thinking if I can talk, breathe and think at the same time, I'm good. I ask my question and stump Kyle right away. Kyle gets to go for the next fifteen minutes or so and then it's Enid's turn. Max seems out of sorts, not answering, not asking, kind of distant.

Taking a few steps backwards, I let Enid and Kyle get out of earshot so I can find out what's up with the man from Dusseldorf.

"I just can't do it," he says. "I feel stupid. I feel inferior."

"Stupid? Inferior? You?" I give Max a little push. "You're the Wunderkind! Remember? You know the answers. They're just locked up there." I give his head a light tap. "Just unlock what's inside. And about feeling inferior, I think it was Eleanor Roosevelt who said something about the only way you can let people make you feel inferior is if you give them permission." I left Max to think about my brilliant words, okay, Eleanor's brilliant words. If only I practiced that concept myself.

Cold feet, it's just cold feet. He'll be fine. In a few weeks we will be sitting at a table challenging the only other team in the state to come close to where we are in the Einstein Challenge. Right before the world gets ready to kill turkeys everywhere, before we celebrate Native Americans trading hospitality for betrayal, is when we will be crowned kings and queen brains.

It's questions, questions and more questions for the next hour and a half. Max and Kyle leave before the sun goes down and I stay behind and help Enid pack up our picnic.

"How's it going?" she asks.

"How's what going?" I wrap the blanket up into a ball and stuff it into her backpack.

"The cousin thing?" She goes to take the backpack from me, but I sling it over my shoulder instead.

"I got it." I pick up the bag of trash and start walking toward her house. "The cousin thing is going okay. Dylan is going to try out for the football team. I'm thinking that's not such a good idea."

Enid chases a stone up the path, kicking it from one side to the other. She bends, picks it up, examines it and puts it in her pocket. "Why do you think it's not such a good idea? Does he like football? Does he want to be on the team?"

"Yeah, he likes football, but I worry about The Oak."

"Oh."

"What if – never mind. I don't even know why I'm talking to you about this." I shift the backpack to my other shoulder.

"You sound like you don't *want* him to make the team. Are you afraid he'll like them instead of you?"

She nails it but I'm not about to tell her that I'm afraid he'll *become* one of them. I'm not fessing up to a girl, especially not Enid! "Nah, it just means I'll have to go to football games, that's all."

"Oh."

At Enid's driveway, I hand her the backpack and watch her walk to her front door. For a minute I wonder what her room looks like. Is Enid a girly girl or more the scuffed, wooden bookcase type? I'm not sure what kind of girl Enid is.

FAT_vs_FICTION@BLOGSLOP.COM

Photos of me: 0

Profile: Round

Friends: 5

PAST BLOGS:

Paradise

Who Wants
Seconds?

Guilt

Lean & Mean

Hog it, Blog it

How come?

Sinners

Find

BBW

*Click here
for more...*

Save the whales

I've seen it all now! Even an upstanding organization like PETA hates us.

They actually had the nerve to launch a campaign with a billboard showing a fat person at the beach (from the back) and in big ass letters it says "Save the Whales -- Lose the blubber, go vegetarian".

I, personally, do not eat green anything. I used to eat boogers but I was only a kid! Now I'm pretty much a meat and potatoes kind of guy, a cookies and cream kind of guy, a peanut butter and chocolate kind of guy. You get the picture.

I'm here to ask, what next? Public humiliation for all fatkind? Next thing you know they'll be petitioning against baby fat. Then you'll have that Spanish milk group going after moms world-wide for breast feeding. Supposedly I was fed mother's milk and got so plump they switched me to formula. I was hungry even then.

What's next?

What if the cotton council came after us 'cause we use so much fabric to make our clothes? And the leather industry will come after us 'cause we need extra long belts to hold up our mongo pants. It's a travesty!

If an organization like PETA is going to single us out, I say let them eat cake and we'll gorge ourselves on meat. I'm here to tell you to order those extra burgers in protest! And while you're at it, get your folks to buy lots and lots of barbeque. Hell, make meatball ice cream and we'll use all the parts of a cow.

Hey, I'm no animal killer, but a fat boy has to eat.

This whale is signing out for today.

346 comments

Tell PETA to blow it out of their blowholes.

Chapter 9

Mom practically runs down the stairs and tosses a partially open box on the couch. "Ricky, look what was delivered today! I got it online for you, on special from the *Sew What Tailors* on my shopping channel."

Shiny white material peeks out of the torn cardboard. I pull at the box flaps and like one of those inflatable rescue boats, a white blanket of fluff expands and practically leaps onto my lap.

"What is it?" I toss the thing back at her as if it's alive.

"What does it look like, Rick?" Mom holds it up by the shoulders. "A parka!"

"It's a mass of wintery white puffy, quilted squares." I tell her.

"It's reversible, too!" She pulls the arms through and flips the jacket inside out. She looks bewildered. It looks exactly the same on both sides.

"What's the point?" I ask.

She pulls the arms right-side-in and holds the parka at arms length. "I don't...um, well, it was on sale."

"I guess that's why," I let out a loud, intentional snort.

"Think of it this way, you can reverse it if it gets dirty!"

"Mom, it's supposed to be *reversible*. Doesn't that usually mean another color, pattern or something? Besides, I can't wear *that!*"

"What do you mean you can't wear it?" Mom floats the jacket onto my lap.

"First of all it's white! Horrifying and really white." I push the jacket off my lap and onto the floor.

"Pick that up, Ricky!" She bends to pick it up anyway.

"It's Rick! I'm not wearing something that's going to draw more attention to me than I already do on my own."

"Oh Rick, put it on. At least try it on." Mom pleads. She hasn't got a clue.

I grab the parka, put both arms in and pull it closed around me. "Mom, I look like the Pillsbury Dough Boy, a giant marshmallow or worse, a polar bear!" I take the jacket off and stuff it back in the box.

"Not wearing it." I lay down the law.

"I've already thrown away your old coat. It was too

small." Mom takes it back out of the box and hands it to me. "This *is* your new winter coat. You can wear it or freeze."

"Oh, Christmas!" I put my hands in my hair and pull until it hurts.

"What's going on?" Dylan storms down the stairs. "Are you guys going at it?"

"Going at it?" Mom smiles at Dylan. "No honey, we were just looking at Rick's new winter coat."

Dylan pulls the coat from the box, holds it up and starts waving it in the air. "Makes a good sail! We'll start calling you *Jibby*"

"Dylan, dear, don't be cruel." Mom pats Dylan on the shoulder, takes the jacket and starts for the stairs. "I'll hang it in the hall closet."

"Hang it in the bathroom for all I care!" I yell up the stairs.

My cousin breaks out laughing. I have to admit, even I feel like laughing.

Dylan catches his breath. "She's kidding, right?"

"Oh, no. She doesn't see beyond the purchase, the steal, the conquest. She sees something, she buys it and thinks nothing of the consequences." I pull a box from the stack near the kitchen. "This box has anti-aging creams that she bought for the future. They've already expired." I pull another box.

"This one is filled with canned gourmet clams. She and Dad are both allergic to shellfish."

"She's whack! Funny, but whacky." Dylan sits back, puts his feet up on a box of canned tropical fruits and grabs the remote. "I have an idea."

"About what?" I say.

"About the jacket." I can see the wheels turning behind Dylan's eyeballs...something maniacal is going on in there.

"What if we make you a walking piece of art? I mean, you're gonna get noticed one way or another. What if we make an intentional statement?"

"Is this another of your 'projects'?" I'm already knee deep in being his project.

"Look, what if we take a can of spray paint and do a big, cool mess of graffiti on the coat. It's a canvas waiting to be exploited! Then, you'll look like –"

"A brick wall? The side of a train? I'm not walking around looking like a vandalized bridge!" I cross my arms. "Absolutely not!"

"Man, listen to me. If we make you stand out, then it's your choice. If you wear that thing the way it is now, for sure you're gonna get comments from those jerks. But if you make yourself purposely get noticed, what can they say?"

He has a point. Not a good one, but a point

nonetheless. What harm could it do? I hate the jacket anyway, and Mom would never know. We could spray one side. I could leave the house with the clean, white side on and as soon as I'm down the block, voila, quick change to the dark side.

"Okay."

"Okay?" Dylan seems surprised.

"Okay, let's do it. I even think dad has some spray cans in the garage." I haul myself off the couch and lead the way.

"See, you're improving already." Dylan elbows me in the ribs. I think I might have even felt it. Maybe this project thing is working?

***

Our covert operation has begun. Dylan sneaks the coat out of the hall closet and we hang it on the school fence, behind the house. I have to admit, it's massive. Massive and stark white. What was she thinking?

Dylan shakes a can of spray paint, the metal balls rolling concentrically from top to bottom. "Ready?"

"As I'll ever be." I stand back to watch the master do his dirty work.

"Let's give you a code name." Dylan looks me over,

head to toe and squats down, balancing himself on his toes. "You like science, you like –"

"Girls!" I offer.

"Yeah, girls. Okay, how about this, E=mc2 over here..." Dylan's hand moves with the rhythm of a composer. He appears to have music in his head, and dances to an imaginary beat. "And over here...R...O...M...E...O."

I watch as big, black bubble letters form, the edges bleed into the fabric, filling white areas with gray. It's not bad. I mean, it's *bad* in the sense that Mom would die a thousand deaths if she saw it, but it's not bad.

"Dylan, you're an artist!"

"Yeah. This is what got me thrown out of school for a week. Nearly went to juvie." Dylan smiles and puts the finishing touches on my new coat.

"Juvie? You almost went to juvie?"

"Yup. I'm a criminal." Dylan says criminal like a madman.

My eyebrows head for my scalp. I'm not sure what to do. He did say the guys he hung out with back home were tough guys.

"Just kidding. Nothing major. Spray painted some trains. They couldn't decide what to do with me. I got sympathy because my mom was so sick and everyone in town knew her. They were talking military school but they didn't want to send me away since I was all she had, so they kicked me out of school for a week. Got thrown off the football team, too." Dylan has me hold a sleeve up so he can spray on some more markings. "Now for my code name."

He sprays the words *Racer9* along the sleeve and hands me the coat. "It should dry pretty fast. My work is done."

"It's great, Dylan. Really." I mean it, too. I've never seen anything quite like it and I'm sure nobody else has either. I'll wear it. And it will be *my* choice to stand out and show off the work of my graffiti artist cousin. "You should sell these. I bet you could make a killing on *eBay*."

"Yeah, Aunt Helen would probably buy one!"

We both have a pretty good laugh at Mom's expense.

FAT_vs_FICTION@BLOGSLOP.COM

Photos of me: 0

Profile: Round

Friends: 5

PAST BLOGS:

Fat vs. Fiction

Who Wants
Seconds?

Guilt

Lean & Mean

Hog it, Blog it

How come?

Sinners

Find

BBW

Whales

*Click here
for more...*

Bananas

Ever notice how many cliches include food?

the apple of my eye; life is a bowl of cherries;
that's just peachy;
compare apples to oranges;
an apple a day;
noone here but us chickens; don't count your chickens before they hatch;
like a fish out of water; plenty of fish in the sea; neither fish nor fowl;
let them eat cake; that takes the cake; flat as a pancake; nutty as a
fruitcake;
rubbing salt in his wounds;
butter him up;
like taking candy from a baby;
hide the salami;
bring home the bacon;
easy as pie; it's a piece of cake;
spill the beans;
that's the way the cookie crumbles; caught with your hand in the cookie jar;
the whole enchilada;
slow as molasses;
no use crying over spilled milk;
he's toast;
he knows which side his bread is buttered on;
the greatest thing since sliced bread;
cream of the crop; peaches and cream complexion;
rolling in the dough;
sow your wild oats;
heard it through the grapevine;
life is like a box of chocolates;
cut the mustard;
cool as a cucumber;
cut the cheese

A guy can go bananas over all these cliches. Makes me hungry...

401 comments

Dude, this is really cheeeeeeeeeeeeesy!

Chapter 10

I'm about to shovel a spoonful of Cocoa Puffs in my mouth when Mom walks by, carrying Aunt Diane's ashes. Dylan is at the sink and his face totally pales when he spots Mom holding the urn.

"I don't know where she'll be happiest?" Mom mumbles, looking around the room.

"Hap—" Dylan can't seem to finish his thought, fumbles for his backpack and goes outside. The door slams shut behind him.

Aunt Diane's ashes have become *topic-taboo*. Dad won't acknowledge that they're even in the house and Mom is torn between spreading them over a 'pretty place in the park', casting them to the wind or keeping them in the house. Frankly, it's a little weird but not something I even talk to Dylan about. As long as Aunt Diane is not in the basement, I'm good.

"Mom, why don't you leave her in the living room?" Nobody goes in there except for company and even they don't go in there. I chug the milk straight from the bowl – one of my favorite things when the milk gets all thick and chocolaty. "Mom, maybe you shouldn't move Aunt Diane around when Dylan is in the room. I think you're freaking him out."

Mom looks right through me. I don't think she hears one word I'm saying. This is her specialty, moving things around people's homes, only she doesn't do it so much here. When Mom has a closing, it's all about the presentation and if she has to call in an expert, she will. I think she's treating Aunt Diane as a new accessory. It's kind of weird.

"Where will she be happy?" She asks.

***

School is about as eventful as a caterpillar in the Pupa stage. It's like the calm before the storm. All I have on my mind is the Halloween party and all Dylan has on his is the football tryouts. I'm glad that's all he has on his mind after Mom's deal with the ashes this morning.

Dylan isn't at all what I expected. He hasn't become one of them yet, but he's definitely in *with* them. The surprising thing is how he hasn't ditched me in favor of the

Jockstraps. I don't get it. Actually, I'm not getting anything these days. No hassle from The Oak, no hassle from my parents, not even Candy's insipid drawings during science class.

Dylan catches up with me on my way to the media center. "Dude, will you come to my tryout today? Coach is ready to see what I've got." Dylan smiles that extra big smile like he's got a secret that you couldn't get out of him even if you set him in a pit of rattlesnakes or stuck giant pins in his eyes.

"I don't like to be around those guys, you know that." I figure I can watch from the kitchen window. The whole fly on the wall thing again.

"Rick, Dude, you gotta be my biggest fan. C'mon!" Dylan is practically begging. "Consider this part of your training, Project."

"Okay, but the minute they say anything, I'm out of there." Truth is I want to see Dylan try out. I want to see The Oak squirm a little. The way Dylan tells it, before he got tossed off the team at his old school, he was second string and didn't get to play much – but that's because the other guy was All State. The Oak wishes he was All State.

Dylan gives me one of his shoulder shots, spies one of Candy's gum chewing friends and spins around to follow.

"You got it. Later. Hey, Heather, wait up."

***

There's more than the usual suspects hanging around the bleachers at the Athletic Field. Coach has Dylan suited up for tryouts. Matt, the second string quarterback at Beckett, was injured while showing off his freewall skills to a RahRah. Tore a tendon and he's in a cast for months. Truth is, nobody seems to care. It's not like he'd ever get a chance to play; at least The Oak makes sure of that. The only time Matt was on the field was during practice, but come time for a game and I hear Matt sits on the bench or helps hand out Gatorade if he isn't behind the bleachers with some cute cheerleader.

I sit off to the side where I can watch both Dylan and The Oak, who is hanging close to the coach. If looks could kill, the Oak would be throwing death lasers at my cousin.

Dylan's on the field and here's my take on it – the boy's got a golden arm! The football is like a rocket launching from his hands. He throws a great spiral pass and Coach is yelling "That's the way to do it!"

As much as I hate sports, bonding with Dad over football has paid off. I get it. I get what's going on and I watch The Oak's face twitch as Dylan throws a forty-yard pass as straight as a zip line. Coach sends some of the guys out there to tackle him and Dylan evades every obstacle with wicked twists and turns, scrambling out of the pocket. He's hard on his feet and tough to bring down. He's a freakin' rock star! Once he's avoided everyone in his way he drops back and throws another forty-yard pass and Coach says as loud as he can, "HE'S OUR MAN!"

I'm amazed at how many people Dylan has come to know in just a few weeks. The guys in the team rush Dylan as well as Candy and her posse. The Oak hangs back a few feet from Dylan, waiting for the new kid to acknowledge him. Oak is, after all, still the big man on campus but I'm thinking his days are numbered. Dylan walks out of the huddle and shakes hands with Oak, but not before giving me the thumbs up. So now I'm living with the new second string quarterback of Beckett High, or maybe even the starter. My cousin could be the new Oak.

***

At night, Dylan is all hyped from getting on the team. Mom and Dad smother him with praise over dinner and Dylan is beaming. After dinner, instead of grabbing the basketball like he usually does, he picks up a football and drags me out back.

"Go long!" Dylan yells as he motions me down the field.

Go long? This I know I cannot do! I barely have a grip on shooting a round ball with any real direction. The shape of the football, I just don't get. Besides, I'm only doing the "Project" thing to keep Dylan's mind off losing his mom and having to come live with us. I don't think he really believes he can change me. I do have to admit, though, that I feel a little different. I mean, maybe I've lost a few pounds but no way am I any thinner. In fact, I'm hungrier than ever, but I keep it in check so he doesn't think I'm a total asswipe.

"Dylan, you're wasting your time," I yell back. "You have The Oak for this now. You have a whole slew of teammates to play with. How about we go back to watching the *Fit* TV for inspiration?"

"You're so funny, Rick. Let's go, my man. It's time for you to learn some new tricks." Dylan throws the football, I dodge and it sails past my ear with a slight *whirr*. Definitely not my thing.

"At least try!" Dylan commands.

"Nah, I'm done, exhausted. You don't know what hard work it is carrying this body around all day. You think this just comes naturally?" I laugh at my own joke.

"I hear you. That's why you should tryyyyyyyyyyyy." Dylan comes over and slams the ball into my hand.

"Hold it like this and just pretend. Don't even let go of the ball. Just pretend you can see yourself sending it down an imaginary straight line." Dylan motions with my arm and whistles as the ball pretends to move smoothly through the air. "See it?"

I almost can, although it's not me holding the ball. I see someone else, someone who thinks like me but isn't me. I can see that guy throwing a game winning touchdown pass. Who am I kidding?

***

I can't really sleep and I'm thinking about all the words that rhyme with Rick. Everything except dick. Tick, nah, too small. I go through the alphabet. Flick, hick, lick, nick, pick, sick, wick. Not too many favorable words rhyming with Rick.

The light from the moon comes through my window, casting an eerie glow on the vending machine costume in the corner of my room. In just days I'll be incognito, my fly on the wall plan will actually come to fruition. I feel like a mad scientist about to launch the greatest experiment known to man. It doesn't get any better than that.

Well, it could get better than that if I didn't have to hide out. Like that could happen.

I think about the name Ricky. Icky, sticky, hickey. Nice one. I can dream, can't I?

FAT_vs_FICTION@BLOGSLOP.COM

Photos of me: 0

Profile: Round

Friends: 5

PAST BLOGS:

*Click here
for more...*

Glut vs. Guilt

I know I have an eating disorder. That's no secret. I mean, if you knew me, you'd look at me and say "that guys got a real problem with food." Sometimes you have to wonder how we got this way?

Tonight I indulged in the sundae of all sundaes. I was at an "Olde Fashioned Ice Cream Parlour" (Sorry, I can't tell you the name 'cause then all you chubby chasers will know where I live.), and there's this thing called "the whole kit'n-kaboodle. I think it's meant for a family of five. Well, I ate it. I ate every bit of the eight ice cream scoops smothered with three different sauces, nuts, bananas, strawberries and whipped cream. Oh, and topped with honey nuts and sprinkles. Every bite was like heaven and that's exactly how I felt eating it. Like I was in heaven.

Now that it's over, I'm here to tell you that the angel on my shoulder, and the devil on the other shoulder, are having an argument. About what, you ask? Glut vs. guilt.

Do I feel guilty? Yes, a little. Okay, a lot.

I mean what's the difference between eating a tripple scoop large cup of ice cream vs. the whole kit'n-kaboodle. Probably a billion calories! But let's be reasonable... how much more damage can we cause ourselves? We'll get a little fatter? I'm already HUGE!

Diabetes comes to mind but do we really think about that crap while we're indulging our sweet tooth? Diabetes, I used to think, was for the old, but there's this girl at school that has a pump for her insulin. She's not even fat! I talked to her and it's way more common in kids than we think. She goes on to tell me lots of what you eat turns to sugar in some way or another. Did I know that? I think not.

Does this mean I have to eat salads?

461 comments

I feel you, man. I once ate a dozen jelly donuts AND an entire box of donut holes. Doesn't sound like much but let me tell you, washing it down with a gallon of milk put the finishing touches on one hell of a binge. Man, I couldn't move!

Chapter 11

The UPS guy is wheeling a huge box into my house. Dylan stands there holding the signature pad and smiling. "This one is for us, Dude."

"Did *we* order something? Did *you*?" I can't imagine what's inside a box as big as the one we are using for my costume. I try to read the contents but Dylan is half way down the stairs, holding the box in front of him like it's a box of cookies. I hear him rip the box open and by the time I'm down the stairs he's pulling metal parts from the packaging.

"What is all this?" I circle the area that Dylan is systematically laying poles, big rubber bands and ... weights. "Weights? Did you buy a weight machine?"

"Yo! You think Aunt Helen will mind? It's all part of the *Project*." Dylan looks up. "It's for you, Dude."

"Wait. Which project? My costume? What's this got to

do with my costume and why would my mom mind? She doesn't care what's down here." It was true. As long as there were places for her boxes and they were neatly placed around the perimeter of the room, she never complained. Of course, she didn't like the idea of her boxes becoming my personal makeshift ottoman, but hey, they're all-purpose boxes! Someone had to find a use for them.

"Well, you said she doesn't notice credit card buys, right? So I, uh..." Dylan goes back to pulling bars and more nuts and bolts from a smaller box.

"You charged this on Mom's card? Are you totally freaking nuts?" I could feel my heart pounding right through my shirt.

"You said she doesn't notice things like your *Wii* buy, right?"

"Dude, that's a couple of hundred dollars. What's this thing cost us? She'll notice *this*." Oh God, I think I'm actually going to faint. I take my place on the couch and hold my head in my hands. My mouth is dry and my heart is beating right the hell out of my shirt. This is it. I'm fat and I'm having a heart attack. Isn't that what happens to really fat people? Breathe. I've got to breathe and get Dylan to put this stuff back in the box and get it out of here before Mom knows anything. We'll get a refund.

My heart resumes its normal rhythm and we stand face to face, well not quite, okay, face to chest with Dylan. "Okay, we can return this, right?" My voice cracks and almost sounds like Enid's.

"Return it?" Dylan stands with his hands on his hips. "Listen, my man, it's only like nineteen ninety-nine a month over, I dunno, a couple of a months, maybe a year or two – but *this* is going to help you get into shape, and me too, while we're at it. Dude, she'll think this is great, don't you think?"

"Who, Mom? No Dylan, I don't think. As a matter of fact, this is something that should have been discussed with me or with Mom first. She's gonna have a cow." Now I'm thinking he used Mom's credit card. How else could he have done this? I go to my desk and look for the paper taped there with the information. He found it. Was he rifling through my personal things?

"Okay, you're gonna tell her, not me. And Dylan, were you going through my things? Were you in my desk drawers?" I stand in front of him now, waiting for an answer.

"Right. Maybe I should have asked –"

"Maybe?" I can't believe it. I pretty much stay below the radar with Mom and Dad and now this. I *will* have to explain this, and I'll have to think pretty fast. "Insanity!"

"What?" Dylan looks around the room as if he's missed

something.

"We'll use the insanity plea. I just don't know how I'm going to tell her you got her card number. Maybe I'll say I did it, and –"

"Insanity plea? Card number?" Dylan looks me square in the face now. "Dude, she has an account. You don't even need a card. You don't even have to talk to anyone. They've got it so that you go by your phone number and that's it...she's hooked up!"

"Really? It didn't used to be that way. Anyway, we'll tell Mom you were, well, are troubled. After all, you just lost your moth – oh, sorry, but we can use it. We'll just say you were feeling really low and this thing you bought is something to, uh, to take your mind off things."

"Works for me. Now help me put this big part up. Hold it like this."

Grabbing hold of the post, I try to show what strength I might have and don't let any amount of banging, twisting or turning move me. I almost have myself convinced that this will work. And hell, when do I ever do anything that goes against the grain. Maybe once, just this once... I look at my costume-in-the-making in the corner of the room and think that if I were to go for this metal workout, maybe I wouldn't have to hide in giant boxes.

For the next hour we're assembling about a billion pieces until finally, the straps are in place and there standing before us is a *Flex-o-Master,* which looks more like a medieval torture device. We admire our work and Dylan grabs all the boxes, papers and left over screws and tosses them into the corner.

"Hop on," Dylan gestures toward the pea-sized seat.

"Are you kidding? First of all, I don't *hop on* anything and secondly, my ass is so huge that thing will disappear." No way was I sitting on something that small. I'd break it or my ass would totally swallow it up. It just wouldn't hold me.

"Dude, this thing holds up to three hundred and fifty pounds. I don't think even you're that heavy. Look..." Dylan sits on the seat and pulls two straps from behind him and alternates arms. "Like this... one, two, one, two..." He lets go and the straps snap back into place with a loud *clank.* He stands and moves away for me to try the equipment.

Suddenly I'm feeling really large. Huger than huge. Gargantuan. I just can't see *sitting* on that thing and making the whole Flex-o-Master fall on my Fat-o-head.

"Just do it. You're being a big baby." Dylan sneers. "Sit!" He commands me like a dog.

"Okay, okay." Obediently, I turn away from the seat and slowly lower myself down. There's nothing to hold onto and my balance doesn't feel quite right, but I'm sitting, I'm actually sitting and the thing hasn't tipped over. At least, not yet. I look at Dylan while trying to hide the amazement in my eyes and he hands me the straps, one and two. I hold them at my sides 'cause I don't exactly know what to do with them.

"Pull, man, Pull!" Dylan yells like a coxswain to his crew.

I pull and it's easy enough. "It's not too hard," I tell Dylan.

"Right, wait till I add some weight." Just like that, Dylan is picking up round, steel donuts and placing them on the machine until I can't pull anymore. My arms feel like they're going to snap off but I can't get my hands free from the pulls.

"Take … it… off," I beg.

"Sorry, Man. Thought your size could handle it." Dylan releases the weights and my arms fly up without any help from my brain. They just rise from the sheer bliss of not having the pull of those weights.

"Baby steps, Dylan. The heaviest thing I lift is my backpack, and most of that weight is my lunch." I say, prying myself off the seat.

"Got it!" Dylan pops the weights on again, sits down and pulls like there's no tomorrow.

"I'm exhausted!" I declare.

"You're a wuss. Go on, get outta here, I'll get you going on this yet." Dylan turns to face the machine and gives a good grunt before pushing downward on a big steel bar.

I go to my room and lay on the bed, listening to the sound of metal scrape against metal, wondering how we're going to explain this to my mom. I can't believe he went ahead and ordered something under Mom's name. Not cool. Maybe if she thinks he really wants to work with getting me into shape, she might just buy it.

I close my eyes and have this vision of me working out and Dylan standing by my side, writing down my progress. I see a chart with a dozen checkmarks and my body becoming defined – not smaller, just buff. It dawns on me that I can be this big and become a muscle head. Heck, I'd be daunting! I could grow my hair real wild, put on one of those stretchy things and make the wrestling world my home. I'd fit in! How cool would that be?

***

"Salad, Dylan?" Mom passes the bowl over my plate into Dylan's waiting hands.

"What if I want salad?" I say, even though the thought

of salad isn't really my thing. I think green things should remain in the ground or up your nose. No point in adding salad to my plate. Just messes things up.

"Well, do you?" Mom raises an eyebrow.

"Uh, no, not right now." I move my potatoes over the plate. "No room."

"All right then, Dylan?"

"Yes, thank you." Dylan loads up his plate with salad and meat. No potatoes. "Watching my carbs. Speaking of Carbs, Aunt Helen, I—"

I know where he's going with this and I'm worried Mom is going to string me up by my thumbs and leave me for the wolves to eat, if there are any wolves in New Jersey. I'll have to look that one up.

I throw a fake cough into my hand, trying to be clever and cough out a *not now,* but he doesn't catch it, or if he does, he doesn't miss a beat. By the end of dinner, Dylan has Mom and Dad cooing about the purchase. He's got them thinking I really am his "Project" and he's going to help whip me into shape. I'm perfectly able to shape myself into a sphere, an oval, maybe even an octagon.

"Aunt Helen, I would have asked you, you know, but I called for the info and it's like they have you on auto buy. I tried to stop the sale but it was useless. I didn't know they were actually ordering the product, but Rick here figured you might like the idea after all."

Smooth, is all I can think. Can't believe he threw me into the mix.

Dylan doesn't let up. "Anyway, Aunt Helen, you know I've got a little money, and –"

"Don't be silly, Dilly!" Mom puts her fingers up to her lips. "Oh! Dylan, I mean. Oh that sounded bad."

Everyone has a good laugh at silly Dilly and we all live happily ever after. Sometimes I wonder who let my parents out of the asylum. They *are* crazy, and they love the idea of having exercise equipment in the house. It's like some great novelty item had slipped from Mom's peripheral *House Beautiful Shopping Network* experience and she's so glad Dylan caught it.

"Let's give it a try after dinner," Dad says.

"Cool." Dylan moves his head in that I-gotta-song-stuck-in-my-head way and shoots me a double-wide grin and a wink.

Downstairs, Dad *attempts* to muscle around with the equipment, with Dylan adding more weight than he lets on he can handle. I have to hand it to Dad, he keeps up with every bit of weight Dylan adds. Heck, even Mom tries it.

"With Dilly – sorry, I mean Dylan here, we have our

own personal trainer!" Mom gives Dylan a big Aunt Helen hug.

Personal trainer. Are they nuts?

FAT_vs_FICTION@BLOGSLOP.COM

Photos of me: 0

Profile: Round

Friends: 5

PAST BLOGS:

Fat vs. Fiction

Lean & Mean

Hog it, Blog it

How come?

Sinners

Find

BBW

Whales

Bananas

Glut

Click here
for more...

Excorcist anyone?

The other night I was watching this old horror movie, The Excorcist, and thought I might have something in common with the girl who gets taken over by an evil being. Maybe I have a demon inside of me. Maybe that demon is controlling my every move, my every thought, my every craving. Maybe, what I need is a priest, or voodoo dude, or medicine man to knock this demon out!

Think of it. Until now, before they super-sized the entire world, food used to be the way to show off, the way to have fun, the way to be hospitable to, I dunno, a bunch of Romans. Talk about indulging! They'd have a huge feast, throw up, and feast some more. Food was an orgy!

Even the ancient Israelites had it right. Huge feasts for everyone.

Imagine this. No forks! No knives! Famished, guests would gorge themselves on the feast before them and not even use a single utensil. Get this, did you know the pinkies up thing came from dipping that finger in salt. Salt was only for the very rich so that whole pinkies up thing became associated with manners. Manners only really started when they invented utensils! Even the poor would imitate the rich with their manners and I'm thinking that's when all hell broke loose. Who knew who was rich and who was poor?

In some cultures it is an insult to refuse food. Some cultures offered a prayer that was a kind of exorcism before eating to keep their food from being infested by the work of evil spirits. Never mind the fact they didn't have refrigeration in those days. Sometimes you just gotta wonder.

I'm thinking of getting an excorcist to cast out the fat demons and see if I don't give up on food. I mean, not entirely. I'm not whack. I just think there has to be a cure for incurable eating. Something tells me it's time for the fat lady to sing, or the fat kid behind the keyboard to step into another world.

I kind of just want to be ordinary today.

527 comments

I got some mojo in my cocoa. Want some?

Chapter 12

The days are growing even colder and Mom beams as I leave the house looking like a giant marshmallow, in her latest shopping conquest. If she only knew what we did to the jacket she'd lay an egg right on the spot.

Half way down the block I drop the backpack and reverse the jacket. Dylan hands me my stuff and stands back to admire his work.

"Remember," he says, "you choose to be noticed." Dylan folds his arms and gives me the nod of approval.

As we get closer to the school I feel something take over. I don't know, maybe this is what cool feels like. Maybe I look as good as one of those hip hop guys on MTV, all that in their fur coats. Maybe I should get gold teeth!

"Should I get grillz?" I try to be all serious so Dylan will think I mean it. Instead, he just slaps me on the side of my head and laughs.

I try putting a little funk in my step, but when I really focus on my body I can feel myself waddle from side to side. Who am I kidding? Pregrets are starting to sink in.

School comes into view and I see Candy, or rather she sees me.

"Romeo!" Candy screams out.

"Oh, she can read." Dylan snorts.

I'm trying to hold on to the feeling of cool. This coat thing is working. I look around and notice more eyes staring at me. Eyes that I'm asking for. The Oak is looking away until Candy yells, "Romeo, Romeo, *what the hell art thou,* Romeo?"

Candy studies my coat for a while and her hand flies to her mouth. She's laughing uncontrollably but stops long enough to point at me, focusing the attention of the other Rah Rah's in her group my way.

Suddenly I don't feel so cool anymore. I think everyone is laughing, and I mean everyone. I feel deflated, as deflated as a fat kid in a fluffy white parka can feel. I start thinking that maybe looking like a giant ice floe might attract a lot less attention – not like the captain of the Titanic had a clue.

"Yo, fat boy." The Oak yells. "Are those your notes? Run out of paper or something?"

Perry Parker jumps in with "E equals MC squared? Is that short for *E*veryone knows you're a *M*oron 'Cause you're *square*? Get it?" He goes on to explain his moronic statement to the masses.

"Good one!" Oak gives Perry a push, knocking him to the ground. Perry pulls on The Oak's jeans and they go into mock-wrestle-mode.

"Fight! Fight! Fight!" The Jockstraps chant robotically.

"Oh, that was brilliant," I say to the skies. I'm sweating. My body is burning up with heat and embarrassment. I need to get out of this thing and I need to get out of it *now*.

"Romeo!" Candy sings over and over again.

"Ignore them," Dylan whispers. "You look great."

"Get real," I say, unzipping the parka and letting it fall to the ground. I kick it toward the garbage can, bend over with an obvious "oomph" and stuff it in. I scan the lawn and see Enid talking to Kyle and Max. Their backs are turned and if they saw what was going on, they didn't show it. I think about going over to them first but instead I head straight for the doors without looking anyone in the eye, straight for the boys room. It sucks to be me.

I look at myself in the piece of metal meant to resemble a mirror. I guess they're too scared someone might crack it, use it as a weapon, and so they put this piece of steel, nickel, or who knows what it is, on the wall. I try to find my face behind the years of smudges and scratches. I find my eyes and get ready to read myself the riot act for even thinking I wanted to invite people to look at me. What was I thinking? What was Dylan thinking? Doesn't he know these guys yet? Does he have any clue as to what they put me through? No. I can answer that for myself. He wouldn't have a clue what it is to be someone like me when he's obviously so much like them. I can't believe I put my faith in him, let him talk me into wearing that coat. Choosing to be noticed! I'm such an ass.

***

The bell rings and I don't move. I'm in a stall reading about how great Wayne Gretzky was on the ice and how there will never be another number ninety nine. There's a drawing of a half-naked girl and an arrow pointing to her boobs with the word *mellons* scrawled across it. Duh. Can guys be vapid, too? It was definitely time to leave the boys room.

I'm late, but I don't care, nobody's in the halls to laugh at me. Mr. Fuentes shoots me a look as I enter the room, I just head for my desk. No need to cause another scene, especially in Spanish.

"Tarde, Senor Ballentine?" Fuentes doesn't wait for me to sit down.

"Uh-huh," I say.

"En espanol, por favor" Fuentes demands.

"Si, Senor Fuentes, yo soy tarde." I mumble, probably missing a few verbs or something.

"More like *re-tard-ay*," someone whispers.

I slink down in my seat and ignore the world for the next four hours and fifty-five minutes.

***

It's my last driving class with Mr. Kay. Driver's Ed is the one class I feel great in, 'cause it's just me and him. Mr. Kay is the closest thing I have to a friend, besides The Einsteins.

"Where's your jacket?" he asks. "Isn't it a little chilly out to be without a coat?"

"Long story," I grab at my stomach fat and shake it at Mr. Kay. "Lot's to keep me warm," I say, thinking about the parka on the ground in front of the school. Mom is going to kill me when I get home, but hey, she knew I wasn't too happy with it when it came in the mail. Bargain shmargain. She's buying me a new coat, or I'll order one off the *House Beautiful Shopping Network* myself. If Dylan can get away with a whole gym unit, I can certainly get away with ordering one husky-sized coat.

"Last class, Rick." Mr. Kay smiles. "Let's go."

Mr. Kay uses his own car for Driver's Ed. It's a burgundy Buick that's big enough for a family of eight. Okay, a small family of eight, but it's a really big car. The thing about it is, I feel good in it. I fit. It fits me. Usually there are four students to a car for class but everyone picked their driving buddies and guess who wasn't part of the in-crowd. Anyway, Mr. Kay said I was lucky to have private lessons. The whole hour and thirty minutes belonged to me and I get to drive the entire time.

"Rick, what do you say we work on parallel parking today? You've got everything else under control." Mr. Kay pats me on the shoulder.

"Okay, where to?" I put the car into drive and pull out of the school parking lot and onto my street. I hardly have anything under control. I try to put the whole parka incident out of my head.

"How about town? We'll go where the tester will take you, run through it a few times and then how about a shake?"

I look at Mr. Kay. "A shake?" Mr. Kay is way fatter than me. Talk about enabling.

"Drive through. It's a test." He clears his throat. "A test to see how you maneuver between those darn talkie boxes and the curbs they set up. C'mon, it's on me. You don't need too much driving today.

"Okay, you're on!" I say with maybe a little too much excitement. I try to take it down a notch. "My dad is always hitting those curbs. He says it's like bumper cars."

Mr. Kay laughs. "Did you book your appointment for the road test?"

"No, but I will. I think I'm ready."

"You'll ace it. Turn left here... stop sign...okay, park over there between the red car and the silver one. You see it?"

"Got it." And I did, too. I parallel parked like I've been doing it all my life. We drove around a few miles and then to the Sonic Burger for shakes, where I drive through the lane like a pro. Didn't hit the curb once.

"Watch this," Mr. Kay says. He moves closer to me, pushes the button to roll down the window, holds his hand over his mouth and in a muffled voice orders two large shakes. He sits back all proud of himself and laughs his head off.

"Are you okay?" I think he flipped his lid.

"Okay? Ha! I love doing that. I love making my voice sound like those boxes on their worst day and you know what the funny thing is, nine times out of ten they get it right. I swear! They get the damn order right." He slaps his knee. I think it's time for Mr. Kay to hit the padded cell. "Pull in here," he points to a spot outside the Sonic Burger.

We suck down our shakes in about five minutes, laugh at our brain freeze, and then it's time to drive back to school. I shake hands with Mr. Kay who assures me the test will be a cinch and that he'll see me on the road in no time.

***

I head back to my locker, gather my stuff and realize it's going to be a cold, albeit short, walk home. Outside there's The Oak checking out my jacket which Dylan is wearing. He had to have fished it out of the garbage, probably to make fun of me, get on the Jockstrap's good side. Now I'm sure Dylan is one of them, probably getting ready to sling some joke at my expense.

"Rick, over here!" Dylan sees me and waves me over. I keep walking.

"Dude!" Dylan runs up to me, the parka flapping like wings. "Dude, they love it. Seriously."

"Seriously? You're all deranged. What were we thinking making a choice to be *noticed*. What was I thinking. Everything is the same as it ever was, Dylan, don't you see that?"

"Uh, no. I see an invitation for you to join the crowd,

not get all bent out of shape about it. C'mon." Dylan turns to go back to them.

"I'm not joining any crowd. Give me the coat, Dylan." I'm about to blow a gasket. "Give it to me." Maybe I'm overreacting but I really don't think I am. Maybe I'm a little on the sensitive side. What I am is a lot confused.

Dylan takes off the coat and hands it to me. I can't quite make out the expression on his face, whether it's sorry, bewildered or downright mean. I tuck the coat under my arm and think about burning it.

"I'm heading home. I'll see you later." The air felt good against my face. I needed it to keep me aware of my mission. Destroy the coat, have some Pepsi milk, a couple of sandwiches and watch Dr. Phil – in that order.

I think again about the party, how I felt it would be like cold fusion to be there, but even greater if *I* was one of them. Now I'm so sure. I mean, I don't think I ever felt like I really wanted to be part of that group, let alone any group, until now. Can you imagine, after all that? I'm totally conflicted. I mean, if Dylan is part of it…

FAT_vs_FICTION@BLOGSLOP.COM

Photos of me: 0

Profile: Round

Friends: 5

PAST BLOGS:

Funny

Sinners

I eat, therefore

Find Cuisine

Big Beautiful

Save the
Whales

Bananas

Glut vs. Guilt

Exorcist

*Click here
for more...*

Diet.tribe

I woke up this morning with a thought -- actually, more than one thought. People on diets are like tribes and their diet is their tribal custom.

I watched this show on Public Television, *Mondo Cane*, and it was all these weird rituals or just ways of life that were truly bizarre. Anyway, one tribe's chief put his bride-to-be in a cage, fed her tapioca until she was fat enough to marry. Can you imagine someone wanting you as fat as you could be?

What *diet.tribe* are you in? Does it have weird customs?

. The Weight Watchers tribe has you do math while you eat tiny portions of food.
. All white foods are forbidden on Atkins, Keto and South Beach. Their totem consists of a fish, a cow and a chicken.
. Nutri-whatever tribe makes you appear in TV ads holding your pants from 10 sizes ago.
. Jenny Craig gives you a tribe of rock star's wives who look hot after eating frozen food.
. The Cabbage Soup tribe insists that you fart out our calories while doing a tribal dance.
. The Grapefruit Diet tribe dances around high acidity while you slim down. The Hollywood Diet tribe comes with a medicine man who can amputate limbs for weight loss and then enhance those lost limbs with fake ones -- not to mention the fat sucking machines.
. Fat Loss 4 Idiots claims to make you lose 11 pounds in one week which will need to come with a medicine man.

What I like about most of these fad diets I've tried is that very few of them expect you to really move. The idea of exercise is exhausting. Can you imagine the energy you need to do both, diet and exercise?

540 comments

Have you tried the Slim Slow tribe? LOL!

Chapter 13

The walk to school is quiet. Dylan doesn't talk too much and I don't want to bring up the whole parka fiasco. I dug an old denim jacket out of the closet and with a hoody I'm warm enough. It's not like winter is knocking down our door. Close, but not yet.

I'm thinking about eating. I'm always thinking about eating, but this time I'm thinking about eating massive, scary animals. Last night on PBS there was a documentary on this tribe who thought consuming an animal would allow them to absorb the animal's spirit, or warrior-like qualities. I like it. I'm thinking of eating a bear so I can stand taller than everyone else and scare them with only a *grrrrrrrr*. Maybe an alligator even. They can attack at mock speed unless the would-be victim serpentines. A cobra. Who isn't afraid of a cobra? I think about what it would be to instill fear, to see someone's eyes totally freaking out on me. I'm thinking I better not watch anymore of Dad's movies or crazy documentaries.

"One more day till the party," Dylan says. "Sure you want to go through with it? I mean, after yesterday –"

"Heck, no. We, I mean, *I* messed up yesterday." I did, too. I brought attention to myself and that was a big mistake, but my plan for the party is the exact opposite. I'm choosing *not* to be noticed. *I should stick to the plan*, I say with some conviction inside my head.

"You didn't mess up, exactly." Dylan says. "I made you wear the coat."

"You didn't make me wear it. You made it better, kind of." I remember feeling something resembling courage when I had it on, that is, until Candy started her Romeo, Romeo crap. And then The Oak and the others just made it worse. "I did it to myself."

Suddenly I'm paralyzed with the thought that if I go to the Halloween party, the costume might not work. Maybe Dylan is wrong about the costume. He was wrong about the coat, that's for sure. Most of the time I feel like Dylan's on my side, like he's got my back, but yesterday I wasn't so sure. I want to ask him why he fished my coat out of the garbage, why he was wearing it. Was he out to humiliate me for

Brownie points?

When we reach the path to Beckett, Dylan nudges me. "Check it out," he whispers.

I feel like I've just crossed over to the dark side. If I were a cartoon character, this is where my head would shake from side to side and you'd hear *warble, warble, warble.* Not only is The Oak wearing a parka which has graffiti spray painted all over it, but so is Candy. I look around and there are people everywhere in coats and jackets that have been artfully sprayed with graffiti, each with their own handle and of course, The Oak has a tree growing right up the back of his coat. Oak waves Dylan over.

"See what you've started?" Dylan flashes a smile. "*Choose* to be noticed."

"What the heck is going on?" I look around and read one person's jacket after the next. "You're like the Pied Piper or something. It's not about me, Dylan, it's you. You put it on and now they all want to be like you."

"Whatever the reason, I think you might want to wear yours, too." Dylan saunters over to The Oak to get a closer look.

Me, I'm no conformist. I try to shake the vision of all these people out of my head and wonder what this place is coming to. Life is just a little too surreal for me these days.

And tomorrow will be the most surreal of all when I'm hanging at a party with the Jockstraps and the RahRahs. Yeah, that's right. Party. I'm going to wear my costume and take a chance, only this time I'm sure Dylan's got my back.

FAT_vs_FICTION@BLOGSLOP.COM

Photos of me: 0

Profile: Round

Friends: 5

PAST BLOGS:

Fat vs. Fiction

Lean & Mean

Hog it, Blog it

How come?

Sinners

Find

BBW

Whales

Bananas

Glut

Excorcism

*Click here
for more...*

Excorcism Redux

Well, no luck finding an excorcist.

I've been trying, on my own, to maybe eat a little less. I mean, I haven't gone completely bizonkers, nor am I able to. I just don't have the willpower it takes to really get motivated.

I stood outside a meeting of Overeater's Anonymous. Funny thing, nobody noticed me. I mean, nobody looked at me at all. As a matter of fact, I looked like so many others waiting to go inside. Still, I just couldn't get my ass in there.

I went home and read their literature. Basically, they'll take anyone who wants to stop eating "compulsively". Their lit says their primary purpose is to "abstain from compulsive overeating and to carry this message of recovery to those who still suffer."

I've seen lost of movies with alcoholics who go on binges and wind up in AA, I guess this is the same. You'd think us fat guys are the overeaters they're talking about but it's far more serioius than that... It's about skinny people, too. It's about dieters who yoyo, about purgers, about people who merely use food as a reward or comfort. There are even people who are addicted to laxatives! Man, taking a dump is so not my problem. It's the stuff goin' in that's the problem!

I overheard one guy say how you can't blame your parents for everything. He said YOU have to take responsibility for who YOU are today. Maybe that's my problem. I have no responsibility for anything, except maybe this blog. That guy was trying to get another guy to come inside. He said one only needs "a little willpower to abstain from overeating."

I don't really like the word abstain. Makes me think I'll never have sex. Actually, who would have sex with me now?

Do I have even a little willpower? Maybe I need to get a job?

527 comments

If sex isn't motivation enough, I don't know what to tell you.

144

Chapter 14

"I don't know, maybe I should go home," I shout through the shell of my disguise. A pungent smell fills the box. It's a mixture of my body odor, my breath and a whiff of the pile of leaves I'm stepping in.

"Whoa, this way." Dylan guides me back onto the sidewalk.

"I feel like Scout in her big ham costume. I can see only what's directly in front of me, pure tunnel vision. Are we there yet?" I ask.

"Another block. Dude, you look great. Nobody will know it's you and once we have you set up in a corner somewhere, everyone will think you're part of the scenery, or if you don't move at all, they'll think you're a real vending machine."

"It's that good, huh?" I feel an ounce of courage return.

"You look freakin' amazing! I'm telling you, if there was a prize for best costume, you'd take it!" Dylan pounces on the box a few times with his fist.

I hear music in the distance and there's a knot in my stomach that grows larger with every step. I take a deep breath and wonder if I'm going to die of carbon monoxide poisoning, breathing in my own exhaled gases. I laugh at the thought of farting in here and what that would do to me, then panic sets in and I can hear the blood rushing in my ears as if I were listening to a giant conch shell in stereo. I suddenly have the need to get out of this box. I've never been claustrophobic but it's not like I ever get myself into tight spaces either.

"Dylan, I'm not feeling so good, I think I need out of here." I break into a sweat.

"Dude, we're almost there. Get it together. Shake it off!" Dylan yells like Coach Mart. "This is all part of the Project. Remember? Eye on the prize. Look at what you did at Beckett. You got all those people to follow your lead with their coats."

"No," I correct Dylan. "*You* got all those people to –"

"This is about you. This is your night, remember that. You got the invite, you're here now." Dylan coaches some more.

My night...my invite...I did get an invite, even if it was

a mistake, it's mine. I'm going to the party and I'm going to have fun if it kills me. What am I getting myself into? I think about turning back, walking away before anything bad has a chance to happen. I'm about to give in to my paranoia when Dylan pushes me up three steps.

"Here you go," he says, ringing the bell.

I turn my body to the left and then turn to the right, trying to catch a panoramic view of where I am. A bloody rubber hand sticks out of the mailbox squeezing a spider so hard its eyes are bugging out, a skeleton has been taped to the door and there are cobwebs all over the windows. The porch is lined with candles and I think about how flammable I must be in this cardboard box. I can see the headlines now: *Fat Boy Stuck In Box Goes Up In Flames.*

The door opens with screaming sound effects and some girl appears dressed as a sexy alien, obviously happy to see Dylan.

Dylan steps directly in front of me. "Hey, Allison," he looks back, raises his eyebrows and smiles at me. "You look out of this world!"

"You know her?" I whisper inside my box, only Dylan can't hear me because they're laughing at his sharp sense of wit. My nose itches only I can't scratch it and it's driving me crazy. Dylan had to put the box over my head with my arms pinned tight to my body. I'm like a penguin stuck in an ice cube, only this one isn't as cold as I'd like it to be. Note to self, next time more air holes. This, I can tell, is going to be one long Friday night.

"Great costumes!" She squeals. "Like, can I have a coke?" She presses a few of my buttons and Dylan holds up a wrench.

"Broken, sorry Martian Girl."

"Ooooooooh, I guess I'll just have to get a drink somewhere else on this planet. Want one? You look thirsty."

"Oh, yeah." Dylan taps the box and whispers, "See ya, fly guy."

I give the room a once over and find a perfect spot against the wall, out of everyone's way, but open enough that I can take in a wide-angle view of the whole party. I waddle over and situate myself where I can see a group of kids standing, close enough for me to eavesdrop on their extra-normal conversation. I can talk like them, so why is it so hard to shoot the shit? I become an unseen part of the conversation about teachers, the upcoming Thanksgiving holiday and occasional laughter. I feel like yelling, 'I'm here!' but of course, I don't. I stand still, witnessing several clusters come and go, each with some boring commentary I secretly want to participate in.

I spy Candy and Audra, both dressed as slutty vampires, both wearing tight black dresses that outline their every curve. They walk right toward me, lean on my box and start giggling. I'm thinking they don't know that someone is in here. They're so close I can smell Candy's shampoo again. My hands are pinned to my side but something else is trying to rise to the occasion. Oh my God! I promised I would go cold jerky on myself, not do the deed until I could actually meet someone but it's not looking so good. The only thing keeping me safe is that I cannot move my arms. *Think bad thoughts, think bad thoughts.* A fresh whiff of Candy fills my nose and sends signals straight to the wrong brain, the not so smart brain, the one I can't control.

"...I did. He took a picture of himself with my phone of me smiling up at him, if you know what I mean." Audra bragged.

"Don't go sexting that or anything, Aud, you'll get in so much trouble." I watch Candy put her hand to her mouth in total shock. "*He* didn't take one of *you* with *his* camera did he?"

"Are you crazy. I'm in control. I'm always in control. That's why I was down there in the first place." Audra flips her hair, mixing the scent of perfume with the intoxicating shampoo that had already taken over my space. "I'm not totally nuts…about Perry that is!"

Candy looks my way and her hand flies up to her mouth again. "Holy shit! Is someone in there?"

I move my head far back into the darkness and hold my breath. Audra looks directly at what would be my eyes but she can only see two candy bars. I can see them, but no way can they spot me.

"Nah, probably a decoration Perry made, or maybe the person inside got tired and left it here." Audra takes another peek just to make sure. "C'mon, let's go find Perry. I'll show you how wrapped around my finger he is."

"I think you got that backwards," Candy squealed. "Slut!"

"Ho!" Audra countersluts.

My fly on the wall scheme was exactly what I wanted. Except for the little episode down below, I'm good. I'm getting a glimpse of the real world. The world I could be a part of if I weren't a…vending machine. I'm kind of hungry and definitely thirsty but there's no way I can eat or drink in here.

The better part of an hour flies by and I'm watching Dylan smooth-talk Allison on the other side of the room. He's got one hand on her hip, casually moving his face closer and closer. Another minute or two and he'll have her kissing him square on the lips. My view of Martian Girl and Repair Guy soft porn is solidly blocked by The Mighty Oak and his buddies.

"Got any change?" The Oak asks one of his obedient Jockstraps.

"You don't need any change. You just gotta kick it!" Another of the Jockstraps barks.

He can't know it's me. Then again, maybe he saw me walk in earlier with Dylan, and then again, who else would be in a refrigerator box disguised as a vending machine.

A giant thud shakes the bottom of the box. My heart literally feels like it's dropped into my pants and I don't dare speak. If the Oak really knew it was me for sure he'd do something obnoxious, something damaging.

"Hey!" Another of the jockstraps jumps in. "Maybe it's stuck." Grabbing hold of my costume by the sides, he starts shaking me. My legs don't have room to bend, I've nothing to brace myself with and nearly rock right out of my sneakers. The motion stops and I stand as far back in the box, trying to lose myself in the darkness again. My fight-or-flight reflexes kick in only I can't do either. This fly on the wall thing really isn't working out.

"What good is a vending machine if there's nothing good inside?" I see The Mighty Oak turn to go but something changes his mind. "See that repair guy over there leaving with

Allison? Let's ask him if he's got any change. I think he's the other half of this costume." The Oaf looks directly into the box and says, "Right, fat boy?" Next thing I know, he spins on his heels, grabs hold of the box with me in it and with a grunt like something out of World Wide Wrestling, topples me to the ground.

I'm stunned – feel like a bird that's been knocked off its perch, you know, the way they just lay there paralyzed with their legs up in the air? Only I can't move my legs and my arm is pinned underneath me. I can't budge even an inch to get it unpinned. I'm immobile, and I think I might even be a little broken. "I'm in here," I whisper. I think about Dad's horror movies, about being buried alive and nobody hearing the voice coming from the coffin. That's kind of how I feel, like one of those people who try to claw their way out, only I can't move my freakin' arms!

Why couldn't they just leave me leaning against the wall, quietly watching. Not like I'm bothering anyone. I let out an internal scream that busts straight through my head. Where's Dylan? Why hasn't he come to kick the crap out of these guys, or hell, get me out of here? He had to have seen it, has to see me lying here now.

I've been in this position for a while now and I really can't see much. I hear things being placed on the box, taken off. At one point I think I smell chips…and maybe salsa. I sniff the air again. Definitely onion dip...no, wait, salsa…no, onion dip. I'm hungry, very hungry. A drink spills through one of the openings. It's like torture as it *drip, drip, drips* onto my forehead, runs down my neck, into the collar of my shirt. Someone tries to sit on me, but I scream out and I'm sure I sent them running scared.

Since there's nothing I can do without giving away my true identity, I manage to pull my arm out from under me and squeeze between the box and my hip. I try to relax. I figure The Oak and his boys have moved on. I get that they know it's me in here but nobody else does and I'm not about to ruin *everything*. I have to admit, the music is pretty good, and I find myself flexing my feet to the beat. Okay, it's not exactly what I had planned when I wanted to be incognito but hey, you gotta make the best of what you got, right? I mean, not like I have a choice.

My view of the popcorn ceiling is getting a little old when I hear a whisper. "You okay in there?" It was a soft voice coming through my cola dispenser. "Hello? You okay?"

"I'm...yeah, I'm okay. Just resting." Awkward. Why can't I just say something normal?

"Resting, huh?" She laughs a soft, girly laugh. Her muffled voice is coming from the display case now. Her voice moves up to the candy bars in front of my face and I see the prettiest eyes I've ever seen – the most unusual pale green eyes outlined with burnt orange rings.

"I'd help you up but I don't think I can move such a big box on my own. Did you come with someone?" she asks.

I have to concentrate hard on the words. I can barely hear her over the music. "Yeah, a guy dressed like a repair guy."

She laughs. "The one with the butt crack?"

"Yeah, that's the one." I laugh too. I was laughing with a girl!

"I'll find him." As quick as she comes into my life, she's gone. Some beautiful cheerleader type was talking to me. Me! Had I seen her before? If I had, I sure didn't notice her eyes. I'd hit myself in the head if I could. For one thing, I avoid all eye contact with everyone at school and for another thing, if I do get to look at a girl, it sure isn't her eyes I'm checking out.

I'm pondering the who's and what's and if's when Dylan comes to the rescue, and with the help of two girls – one being the one whose face he was eating – stand me upright. I didn't see who the other one was but I made a vow then and there I would have to find her.

"Dude, you okay?" Dylan whispers into the box. I smell alcohol on his breath.

"I'm okay, now. Thanks." I'm standing and the blood rushes back to my arm, legs and feet, where it belongs. Horizontal is good, but not so good for parties – at least not this kind of party.

Truth is, I didn't expect Dylan to hang around me but I also didn't expect the Jockstraps to ruin my night. Who am I kidding? The Oak knew it was me and I knew deep down coming here would be trouble, but now I think maybe it was all worth it. Those green eyes are stamped on my brain and I didn't even get a chance to find out who it was. It was probably one of Candy's friends, one of the cute girls from the cafeteria. Does she know who I am? Does she know it was me, the fat boy in the box?

Once we're a few blocks from the party, Dylan lifts the costume off of me and we ditch it in a dumpster. It feels unbelievably good to be free. I stretch my hands high over my head and attempt to bend over and touch my toes. I feel like a sausage that's busted out of its casing. I hang suspended over my toes for a while and slowly straighten up.

"Man, by the time I got to you, you were covered with drinks and someone even planted a plate of weenies on you!" Dylan laughs.

"Real funny." My cousin definitely had a few drinks. His speech is all messed up and his eyes are all glassy. "Where were you while I was a human coffee table?" I ask.

"Off with Allison. Or should I say, getting off on Allison," Dylan laughs, throwing him slightly off balance. He fixes his hair with his hand and stands straight so I won't notice.

"Already? Do you even know her?" Suddenly I sound like my father.

"Of course I do. She sits next to me in biology." Dylan kicks at the ground. "Hey, you don't mind if I go back there, do you?"

Mind? If I had to chance to go back there I sure would. "No, you go ahead. I've got bigger fish to fry."

"You are a true friend. You're the man!" Dylan spins on his heels and is gone before I can say another word.

I'm the man. He's not! True friends don't leave friends to go back to a fun party when the other friend has to leave. That's not what friends do. Well, at least I think that's what I think, not like I have a ton of experience in the world of friend and party protocol.

I head back toward my house, away from the party, away from the almost-perfect costume, away from those pale green eyes. A blast of wind kicks up and for the first time I notice the leaves on the trees are nearly gone. I dig my hands deep into my pockets hoping to get a little warmth going. It was warmer when the cardboard box kept all my hot air inside. Now the wind was biting at my flesh, forcing me to walk faster. By the time I get home my blood is pumping and the cold air on my face makes me feel strangely alive.

I start for the door to my house, but instead of going home where a triple-decker sandwich, some Pepsi milk and probably a hunk of chocolate cake awaits me, I detour around back. I maneuver my way through the hole in the fence and I walk. I walk two times around the track and I walk fast. I pretend the girl with the green eyes is waiting for me and my racing heart at the end.

FAT_vs_FICTION@BLOGSLOP.COM

No sugar, no calories, no taste

I went to the supermarket with my mom today and she kept pointing out all these "new" products that have no sugar and only 100 calories or less. There is a goldmine out there for people who make food.

Everyone thinks they're fat.

Even thin people think they're fat. Mom thinks she's fat and you don't even see one roll on her when she sits down. Her stomach is flat and smooth. Dad, well, he can use to lose a few. I think I got it from his side of the family. But seriously, everyone does think they're fat and they're buying up this 100 calorie stuff like it's going out of style.

What they don't tell you is the stuff that's inside those little bags is barely enough for a snack. Sure, I let mom buy several boxes of cookies, pretzles, protein bars, but then I eat the whole box! What's the point? So now I know I ate 800 calories in one sitting 'cause they've counted it out for me?

I try, guys, really I do. I buy low fat turkey and wind up eating the pound in one sandwich. I buy diet soda which leaves such a foul aftertaste that it leaves me craving for real sugar. Craving! That's it, I'm a junkie. A sugar junkie. Now, aren't I supposed to feel better 'cause I admitted it?

Maybe I will go to that Overeaters Anonymous meeting. I can stand up and say hi, I'm the blogslop guy and I love sugar. Then they'll all say hi blogslop guy and try to put their arms around me but they can't 'cause I'm so fat!

Look, it comes down to this... If you're going to take the sugar and the calories and the fat out of something like a Devil Dog, then what you're left with essemtially is a hologram of something that looks the same but in essence isn't real at all.

I might as well just go to the kitchen, pour a bag of sugar down my throat and be done with it. And I'm not going to the supermarket with my mom anymore. That's a promise.

627 comments

Sugar is your friend. That other stuff has been linked to cancer.

Photos of me: 0

Profile: Round

Friends: 5

PAST BLOGS:

Funny

Sinners

I eat, therefore

Find Cuisine

Big Beautiful

Save the Whales

Bananas

Glut vs. Guilt

Exorcist

Exorcist redux

Click here for more...

Chapter 15

Saturday morning, I get up before anyone else in the house, go back through the hole in the fence and walk as fast as I can around the track. I have to play games, like if I make it to the second tree I have x amount of points and if I make it past the gym door I'll get a date with the girl with the pale green eyes. I'm so out of breath and have to stop every now and then. My legs cramp up but at the same time there's a warmth building deep within my muscles, that's strangely comforting. If I make it through a whole lap I'll reward myself later with something wonderful to eat! Okay, maybe that's not a good reward, but maybe I can *pretend* there's a food reward at the end. Hey, whatever gets me through, right? My goal is five laps before the sun fully lights the sky and back home before anyone knows I was gone.

I replay the party in my head and wonder where I went wrong. I think in some weird way it actually was a success because I did what I set out to do. I was there! I had the invite, I had the costume and I went to the ever-so-popular Perry Parker's party. In some sideways kind of way, I even met a girl.

Back at the house I flip on the shower. My calves hurt from walking. What I wouldn't give to lie down in a tub and soak in a bath. A bath! Even showers are a chore, lifting my flab, making sure every fold of flesh is clean. I let the hot water wash over me and grope at the soap dish with my clumsy fingers. I stare as the bar of soap slips from my hand and falls to the tub, sliding in slow-mo from one end to the other. I make a mental note of not stepping on it since picking it up is not an option.

I twist open the shampoo and pour it into my hands. It will have to do as body wash, too. Soaping up my body I'm aware of every roll, every bit of myself and who I am, who I was before Dylan came to live with us and most of all who I don't think I'll become.

I think of all the Jockstraps at school and how they mob the showers after class, joking with each other, talking about upcoming games. Dylan will be one of those guys. I think of how it would be to be in there like one of them, and then I think how for once it would be great to just not be noticed as opposed to ignored.

I get out of the shower and look down at where my toes should be, convinced I can see a sliver of toenail. Maybe a few laps and Dylan's Torture-o-Matic can make a difference. Maybe being Dylan's project isn't really such a bad thing after all.

Making sure nobody sees me up this early, I go back to my room and get into bed. I fall asleep and dream that I opted for Home Ec instead of gym class. I thought it would be about food, baking cupcakes, rolling out pizza dough, being domestic. What I got instead was a sewing project which wouldn't have been so bad had it not been a *poncho*. And, add insult to injury, the fabric was chosen for me. No kidding! A hot pink plaid number and here's the final kicker, the poncho had to be worn in a class production for a final grade. It was bad enough having the girls in class help me thread my bobbin, but I begged Ms. Markham, the Home Ec teacher, for clemency. Told her I would do anything she asked of me if she didn't make me wear the poncho in the stupid production. Ms. Markham, a member of Mensa, made me promise to kick ass in the Einstein Challenge. She later reneged and told me I had to participate in the catwalk at lunch. I was about to follow the girls into the cafeteria and woke up in a serious sweat.

I thank the universe and all the Gods in it that it was all

a dream.

Today, I'm all about relaxation since I exerted every ounce of strength I had on my laps this morning when I hear Dylan clunking down the steps to my lair.

"Dude," Dylan flies off the last step. "We're going to make a little mischief tonight!"

I'm perfectly settled on my couch, eating the usual lunch sans one less sandwich, feet propped up on a box of pickled asparagus and truly going nowhere. Cabbage Night was the night I hated most, because it was me who would have to get up the next morning and take down all the toilet paper from our trees and bushes. One year they even went as far as tying our doorknobs together so we couldn't get out the front door. Man, Mom was on a rampage that day. She called each and every mother in the neighborhood and chewed them out for not having better control of their children. I believe, that day, I was a saint.

"I don't indulge in mischief," I say. "I'm the cerebral type, remember?"

"The guys at the party make it sound like playtime compared to what goes on in Detroit. I think we started

Mischief Night. It got so out of hand at one point they had arson everywhere. It was so bad they had Angels, like neighborhood watchmen out there, watching our every move. It was crazy! The city would look like it was on freakin' fire." Dylan paces around the room, sits on the Torture-o-Matic and fits his hands into the straps.

"You set fires?" I am slightly afraid of my cousin at this very minute. I can see the headlines now...*Jock turns out to be serial arsonist, burns down Merryweather, New Jersey.* Then Dr. Phil will have my mom on his show and she'll say how she didn't know, how he was such a *nice boy.*

Dylan adds more weight and pulls till the veins on his arms started to bulge. "No, not me, no way. But I knew plenty of guys who took it to the max. They'd go to all the tent cities and terrorize the homeless. That's where I drew the line. No way was I hurting those guys, but a little mischief in the neighborhood, that's okay. We didn't hurt anybody, really."

"You think? Even TP'ing someone's house is hurtful. I ought to know." I flip the channel – nothing on Sundays except for a bunch of religious stuff. I settle on Sponge Bob. How old do you have to be to give up Sponge Bob?

"C'mon, Rick. It's time for you to hang out and socialize."

"Dylan, I didn't socialize before you were here and I'm

sure as hell not going to start now. The last time I socialized I was tipped over and used as a table. Oh yeah, that was yesterday. You know how those guys are? Besides, I'm not causing any mischief. I don't consider that socializing."

"*Bawk, bawk, bawk, bawk!* Chicken!" Dylan starts dancing around the room, sticking his neck in and out like a rooster.

"Sticks and stones, Dude. I'm good."

I thought that would be the end of it until Dylan told Mom and Dad at dinner that we were heading out for some fun. Of course with Mom's encouragement, I suddenly find myself standing on the corner of scared and shitless with a bunch of the Jockstraps. They're all dressed in black jeans and black hoodies. I guess I didn't get the memo. My lime green hoodie is practically neon under the streetlights.

"What's he doing here?" The Oak gives Dylan attitude.

"He's with me," Dylan says.

Me, I don't say anything, but I don't hang my head either. I'm thinking that he was a dick at the party last night, but what did I expect, really? He and his jackass brigade knocked me down. I can almost feel my temper boil and then I remember the girl with the light green eyes. If it weren't for The Oak turning me into a coffee table, I might have never met her.

Perry Parker looks around and heads straight for me. I'm about to piss in my pants but instead of doing anything to me, he hands me a twenty dollar bill.

"You are going inside of Kendal's and buying us a few dozen eggs. They won't sell to us, but they'll sell to you." Perry smiles.

"I know Mr. Kendal. I'm not going in there. He'll know what it's for." I can't believe I'm denying Perry. I am probably going to have my head bashed in another minute but the Kendals know my parents, too.

"That's exactly it, Rick. He won't think twice about selling *you* eggs. He'll think you're bringing them home to mommy." Perry steers me in the direction of Kendal's flashing "open" sign.

"Go," he commands, pushing me toward the crosswalk.

I walk slowly toward Kendal's and by the time I put my hand on the door I'm shaking in my shoes. I swallow hard and pull on the handle. The bell rings and Mr. Kendal looks up from the TV.

"Hello, Rick. What'll it be?" Mr. Kendal smiles.

I need a quick lie. "Oh, Mom is making cakes for an open house and sent me for some…eggs. I need a few dozen." I'm not sure what it takes to make a cake exactly but I'm sure it doesn't take more than a dozen.

Mr. Kendal raises an eyebrow. "Looking for trouble, Rick? I can call and check, you know."

I can't believe this is happening. What am I, five? I look at Mr. Kendal and try to convince him with my eyes that there is no way in hell I, Rick Ballentine, would be looking for any kind of trouble.

"M-m-m-me, Mr. Kendal?" I stammer. "You know me. I don't have any use for eggs *that way*. When have you ever seen me do something wrong?" I start to feel a little better about lying because I'm not lying about the last part, the part about me ever doing anything wrong.

"I'm sorry, Rick, you just don't know who to trust these days. You're a fine boy. Sure, take what you need. Tell your mother to bring me a piece of this cake she's making."

"Yes, sir!" I say, carrying the eggs outside.

I don't see the guys, only an empty street. I look up the block and there's Dylan, signaling for me to come. I can't run with the eggs. Hell, I can't run without them either! All I can think is *don't drop the eggs, don't fall, don't mess up, don't drop the eggs*. Something wicked this way comes, jumps into my head. *Something wicked* loops in my brain over and over again until I hand the eggs over to Perry.

"Good boy, Rick."

I'm waiting for a pat on the head and a dog biscuit.

The Oak jumps out from behind a tree with rolls of toilet paper. "Let's get started!"

From this point on it's a blur. We run from house to house, TP'ing the trees, the bushes, the driveways. The Jockstraps smash the already rotting pumpkins that have been sitting on porches for weeks before Halloween. Windows of cars have messages scrawled on them with bars of soap, and in some cases on front doors. The Jockstraps have gone wild. It's like they've been let loose to do as much damage as they possibly can, knocking over mailboxes and pulling down decorations. Part of me feels like this is so wrong, *knows* it's wrong, but the other part of me, the me wanting to be cool thinks this is great, being one of the guys.

They run and I hide. I can't keep up with them but each time some unsuspecting family opens their door to see what all the noise is about, their expression is the same. I see the desperation on their faces that I used to feel on mine when I saw what acts of vandalism were committed on our house. The eggs, given time to dry, were like glue and tough to remove.

When all the toilet paper, soap and eggs are gone, they resort to the old Ding-Dong-Ditch, ringing doorbells and running away.

One house has no place for me to hide, not a tree or bush in sight. It's one of those houses most definitely owned by a family from another country. They chose not to have a lawn, just a cement plot with statues and giant urns everywhere. The Jockstraps topple the statues, ring the bell and split, leaving me totally exposed.

"Here, Barfy! Here, Barfy!" I call out.

"What you are doing there?" The man at the door yells in a thick accent.

I look around. "Me, sir? Looking for my dog."

"You lie. You have no dog!" The man takes steps toward me. "I call police!"

Call the police? Oh god! That's all I need and you know it won't be hard to find me once he gives a description of a very fat boy who can barely run, let alone waddle straight. Now I'll have a record. They'll probably put me in Juvie and there goes my future. I look at the man with the saddest face I can make.

"No, really, sir. I *have* no dog because I *lost* my dog. If you don't believe me, you can call my mother..." I was hoping that would get him off my trail. "I can give you her numb—"

"I think I see him over here!" Dylan yells from two houses down, coming to my rescue.

"Oh! Excuse me, sir." I turn on my heels and actually

run, well, waddle down the block. By the time I reach Dylan, I'm winded as all hell and can hardly breathe. "I'm...done...going...home." I manage to get the words out.

"I'll go with you. We're pretty much finished here." Dylan looks around to make sure the man isn't following us and we head back to the house. I'm still trying to catch my breath by the time we make it to our door.

"That wasn't so bad, was it?" Dylan asks.

"Was what?" Is he talking about having to hang out with a bunch of imbeciles? Is he talking about the humiliation and guilt of ruining people's homes? If I didn't want that to be done to me, why would I do that to someone else's property? But there's that wanting-to-be-cool me that is just this much happy that I was part of *something*. Then I realize this is the first year our house isn't a rainforest of toilet paper. There is no egg on my door, no shaving cream on the car windows. Nothing.

FAT_vs_FICTION@BLOGSLOP.COM

Photos of me: 0

Profile: Round

Friends: 0

PAST BLOGS:

Hog it, Blog it

How come?

Sinners

Find

BBW

Whales

Bananas

Glut

Exorcism

Exorcism 2

No sugar

*Click here
for more...*

Fire the help!

I'm mad. I'm so mad I punched a hole in my bedroom wall.

Mom got rid of Magda, our old housekeeper. Okay, she didn't exactly get rid of her, Magda went back to Brazil. She decided it would be better than having immigration do it for her.

Man, I loved Magda. Oh, not romantically, no way, but she was like a second mom to me, and now we've got some crazy Russian lady who barely speaks english and who SOLD ME OUT!

Yes, friends, I'm here to tell you she sold me out. Okay, I don't know about you but I've got a stash in my room that my folks don't quite know about. That stash is located in three separate places: the chips stash, the chocolate stash and the miscellaneous stash.

First of all, I can't believe she would clean my room that thoroughly. I mean, Magda never did, or if she did, she protected me! She'd never rat me out. This one puts all my food in a laundry basket and sets it down in front of mom.

Well, I don't need to tell you all hell broke loose. Mom has forbidden me to eat anywhere in the house other than at the kitchen table. No eating in front of the TV, no eating on my bed, no eating in the family room. The kitchen table is the only place and mom wants me to start writing everything I eat down.

I told her it doesn't work. I tried that Ruben method and it didn't help one bit. So she and dad start fighting about how it's their fault I'm like this and what can they do. They say things like I'm too far gone for help at this point and destined to be fat the rest of my life. Next thing you know, they'll have an intervention, like those guys on TV that are on the edge of hopelessness and in comes the family, the friends and the camera crew to tell him there is hope.

I say fire the Russian and let's get Magda back.

642 comments

Man, that's low.

Chapter 16

Sunday morning I sneak out again. I am possessed, I'm sure. Why I would wake up early, get fully dressed, walk laps around the track, sneak back into the house and shower before anyone is even up, is beyond me. It's not like I even planned this. It's like I'm on a mission, and believe me, missions aren't my strong suit. The only thing I really stick to besides eating is the Einstein Challenge. It's the one thing I can do better than anyone else. The thing of it is, I don't really want anyone to know what I'm doing – in case I fail at whatever it is I *am* doing. In case I really don't stick to this.

Who am I kidding? I'm not thinking I'm going to lose a tonnage of weight. Truth is, I haven't thought of it at all. Something on the night of the party just took over and I have this *void* that's much bigger than my stomach that needs to be filled. And here's the thing of it, I almost like the walking. My head gets really clear and I'm not thinking of anything else except for getting to that next tree, or window, or whatever landmarks I've set for myself as goals. I just *need* to do it.

***

Mom takes us to the mall so Dylan can get a new pair of sneakers. I only go with them because my favorite Chinese restaurant is there and Mom promised we could go. Walking into Wok Crazy, I'm filled with dish envy when I see what everyone has on their table. Mom and Dylan both order Asian salads with extra mandarins. I order the orange beef, the shrimp dumplings and an order of eggrolls. Eggrolls are as close as I get to vegetables and I'm about to dip mine in some hot sauce when the waitress asks if we need anything else. I swear they're trained to do that just when you have a mouth full of food so you can't complain. I look up at her and something about her eyes catch me off guard. I knock the soy sauce clear across the table and nearly send Mom's iced tea sailing into oblivion. They weren't *the* eyes, the pale green eyes, but they were green nonetheless and my stomach lurches.

"What's gotten into you, Rick?" Mom would have whipped out a thermometer if she had one. "I swear, you're all jumpy today."

"Huh?" I put the eggroll down. I actually don't feel like eating. Oh my God! Where is that thermometer?

"Dude, you're staring at your eggroll. You okay?" Dylan looks at Mom. "He's in the land of Catatonia. Want me to wake him?"

"Very funny." I wipe a spot of soy sauce off my hand and stand to go.

"Rick, we're not finished with our salads!" Mom stares at me like I've got two heads. "You guys eat. I'm going to walk around," I say. "Meet you at the Sports Shed."

Maybe I am getting sick. Maybe I am coming down with some rare disease. Maybe I've had a rare disease all along and that's what made me so fat! My stomach feels weird and I need to get some air. I leave the mall, start walking and before I know it I'm back near the school, close to my house. I call Mom on her cell so she won't worry.

"We've been looking all over the mall for you!" She seems a bit on the angry side.

"Sorry, I just needed some air. I'm not feeling too good." I wasn't lying. All I could think of was my bed and the fact that I needed to lay down and bury myself deep under the covers. But first I needed to get to a scale.

"Can I get you something?" Her voice takes on all the charm of a mommy. "Should we come home now?"

"No, you guys have fun. I'll be in my room. I'll take an antacid or something."

"Okay, we'll see you later." Silence. "And Rick, I love you."

"I know, Mom." I roll my eyes. She can be so, well, so motherly sometimes.

This was it. I take off all my clothes and stare at the scale. Right about now I am wishing I had one of those heavy duty scales, like the ones out front in the supermarket, the one I'm always tempted to get on but fear that I'd become a circus act and draw a small crowd. No, no crowd here. Just me and the scale.

I place one foot on the black, rubbery surface and then the other. I can hear the scale cry under the pressure of my weight as the digital numbers change a little too quickly to just below the two sixty-five. I let out a deep breath, the one I've been holding for the last minute or so. *Oh God, what have I done?*

I don't know how long I've been sitting here on the bathroom floor, naked, or how I even got on the floor. I lean over and turn on the shower, just for the noise, for the distraction. I have lost some weight since Dylan came to live with us. The project idea is okay but I need to do something more. I need to take responsibility for who I am *today*. Nobody can fix this except me.

"Rick, Honey, is that you?"

Mom? She's home.

"Uh, yeah, I'm in here." I hoist myself up off the floor and pull my T-shirt over my head. "Sorry, I needed to, uh, wash up." Lame. I would never use my parents bathroom but that's where the scale is. I get the rest of my clothes on and manage to get by Mom without looking her in the eye. She knows I'm lying about something. She always knows by my eyes if I tell even the smallest of lies. Truth is, except for buying things off the TV or online, there is nothing I would even try to get by her.

Downstairs I start to think about what I can do. I mean, it took me sixteen years to get this way. It's not like I'm going to drop down to a thirty-two waist overnight. I have to do something though, but what? A feeling of dread washes over me as I think about all the fad diets I have tried before. This time something has to stick. What was it they said about twenty-one days? Twenty-one days to make a habit stick. Salad for twenty-one days? Perish the thought!

I am Dylan's project though. Dylan can help me. I'll shoot hoops…I'll learn to run, okay, walk fast…I'll eat what he eats…I'll use the exercise equipment. Who am I kidding? Dylan's on the football team now. He won't have time for his

Project anymore.

I sit on the exercise equipment, grab two bands and start pulling. Truth is, I don't even know what I'm doing. That sense of doom rushes over me again. Is this what it will take? Maybe I could call Dr. Phil and we could discuss my 'problem'. Then again, would I want to be on national television as a fat freak high school geek? No. That's better suited for Jerry Springer. Then my mom and dad could fight over whose fault it is and suddenly we'll find out that I'm not even Dad's kid and I've got an illegitimate sister who is also fat!

I switch out of my jeans and into sweats. My sweatpants feel good and I wash my face to see if it makes me feel better. It doesn't. I crawl into my bed, shut my eyes and I'm pretty much down for the night. Don't even eat dinner.

***

Mom's really worried, so worried in fact that she's sitting at the end of my bed when I wake up Monday morning for school.

"Ricky?" She rubs my back.

"Mmmm?" I don't like to talk to anyone in the morning.

"You okay for school today?"

"Mmm hmm."

"Okay, I'll fix you some breakfast."

I push my face into the pillow. "I'll take care of it, Mom. Don't worry. I feel fine."

I did feel fine. I felt like my old self. "Must have been one of those twenty-four hour bugs. I'm fine, really." I pick my head up and look Mom square in the eye so she knows I'm not lying.

"Okay. I'll see you upstairs."

FAT_vs_FICTION@BLOGSLOP.COM

Photos of me: 0

Profile: Round

Friends: 5

PAST BLOGS:

I eat, therefore

Find Cuisine

Big Beautiful

Save the Whales

Bananas

Glut vs. Guilt

Exorcist

Exorcist redux

No Sugar

Fire the Help

Click here for more...

Last man standing

There is nothing more humiliating than being made to participate in team sports and having team captains choose their teammates. Nothing more humiliating than being the last man standing. I mean, it's okay if you're the last man standing in war games, but seriously, it's obvious nobody wants me on their team.

They won't even excuse me from gym class. Unless you're missing a leg, have one lung, or something like that, you have to play.

So, I'm standing there while everyone snickers and has a good ol' time. Then the team that gets me let's out a big, awwwwwww and makes me feel like crap. I mean, WTF?

What ever happened to politically correct? Or doesn't that apply to us fat people. Oh, excuse me, horizontally challenged people. What about the old A, B, kind of choosing, or names in a hat, huh?

I know, I'm far too mad for blogging today. Usually I'm my happy self. Except for that last blog where my housekeeper ratted me out.

They're keeping the housekeeper, btw. Sucks. She's completely changed the house to a barracks. Even my dad can't put his feet up on the coffee table anymore 'cause the Russian goes ballistic and Mom's under her spell. Mom thinks she's the best thing to happen to the house and that Magda was lazy. I tell you, my world is turning more bizarre by the minute.

I have found a way to hide some food though. I've got a stash tucked between my neatly folded clothes. I figure if it's neat, the Russian won't look there, right? I'm pretty smart.

702 comments

I've got a cooler in the back of my closet behind my shoes. Used to keep food under the bed but the dust bunnies got to it before I did. Aaack! Nothing worse than wiping dust off an iced cookie. Think I'll move my cooler.

Chapter 17

Monday morning all anyone can talk about is the party. Evidently, it went on far into the night after everyone left Perry's house. Locker conversations reveal who kissed who and something about going into the woods at Woodland Park. It seems Candy Sapperstein could rival Lindsay Lohan when it came to drinking and some other things. I was dying to know what the other things were.

I feel different somehow, sort of mysterious. I worry that people know it was me in the vending machine costume but nobody says a word to me. It's like I'm still Rick the fat kid only I'm invisible. Walking through the halls I find myself wanting to make eye contact with all the girls – usually I avoid every stare by keeping my head down, but today I don't want to keep my head down. Today I want to find the girl with the pale green eyes.

In science I'm sitting next to Candy and I realize I don't even know what color her eyes are. It's not like it ever mattered to me. Before looking at her, I mean really looking at her, I try to guess. Are they blue? Are they hazel? Are they pale green? My heart starts to race at the thought that it's Candy. Not because that would make me happy. On the contrary, it might just make me ill.

"Hey, Candy, got a pen?" I say, tucking mine in my back pocket. I look into her eyes and am relieved that her eyes are brown, dark, dark brown. "Never mind," I say. "I've got one."

At lunch I scan the gumalicious group and look at Candy's posse. Blue, brown, brown, brown, blue, brown. No pale green eyes in that crew. Sara Boyle catches me checking them out. If looks could kill, I'd be one dead fat boy.

The only other group of girls I can imagine having been at Perry's party are the foreign exchange students. They're just as beautiful as Candy's girls, but too smart to hang with the RahRahs. They do, however, date the jocks and would have definitely been at the party. I try to think if the girl with the pale green eyes had an accent but it was hard to hear over the pounding bass. I'm just not sure.

Dylan walks up, throws an arm around my shoulder. "This weekend, my man, we are going to do something crazy!"

"Crazy?" I'm not exactly the type to do anything crazy.

"Perry Parker dared the football team to go polar skinny dipping. I'm taking you with me."

"Me?" I feel sick. Why would I want to go polar skinny dipping? "Are you out of your mind, cousin? And besides, I'm not part of the football team. Mischief night was enough. I didn't really want to be a part of that either."

"Dude, you don't have to do anything. Just come with me. It will be fun!" Dylan drops his arm and takes off down the hallway after the girl from the party. I'm guessing she's his girlfriend now. It didn't take Dylan long at all to go through the phases.

Phase one: Get in with the Jockstraps.

Phase two: Get a girlfriend.

Phase three was coming: Ditch Rick.

I push the skinny dipping out of my head and move quickly to Mr. Kay's car. Today is my road test and nothing gets in the way of that. Not skinny dipping, not the Einstein Challenge, nothing.

***

I ease into the seat of Mr. Kay's burgundy Buick. You

can always tell when he's got a new air freshener, it's sickeningly sweet. I crack the window a little, snap the seat belt into place, adjust the mirrors and turn on the ignition.

"Thanks for taking me, Mr. Kay. Mom was supposed to but she had to help someone out with a closing." I feel like I'm rambling. I might be just a smidge nervous.

"You're ready, Rick. Probably the best student driver I've ever had." Mr. Kay adjusts the mirror on the passenger side. "Can you see okay like this?"

"Yup."

"Okay, take her out, slow and steady." It's always the same few words whenever we're ready to hit the road.

"So what kind of car are you thinking about getting, Rick?" Mr. Kay burps and twists open a pack of Tums, pops two in his mouth and points out that he has some mean indigestion.

"Something sporty. Of course, I don't think I could really fit into something sporty." I snort. Laughing at myself is way easier than someone laughing at me. "I saw a TR7 for sale in the classifieds for five hundred bucks. I have about that much saved up. What do you think?"

"That's an old car. Besides too much work." Mr. Kay laughs to himself. "You know what they used to say about the old TR7 back then? *Trouble and Repairs Seven days a week.*"

I pretend Mr. Kay's wit is hysterical. He's such a cornball.

"Forget sporty. You want something solid, like this Buick. If I didn't need it for giving lessons, I'd sell it to you. I've got another car at home, you know. This one is solid, though, solid." Mr. Kay pops two more Tums in his mouth, eases back into his seat and shuts his eyes. "You know what to do. Take her to the test course, I'm right here if you need me."

I like that Mr. Kay has so much faith in me. I don't like that he's starting to snore but what the heck, I can do this! I ease the car out of the parking space and onto the road in front of the school. I turn on my left blinker and wait at the stop sign for some old lady to make up her mind and decide which way she's going. I would lay my hand on the horn if I had any nerve, but I don't want to wake Mr. Kay. Another driving school car is on the road and riding parallel with me. I turn left, he turns left. I head out to the driving course and so does he. I stop at the intersection for a four way stop and he sails right through, nearly crashing into a car that clearly had the right of way.

"Did you see that?" I say.

Mr. Kay groans, rubs his belly and motions for me to keep moving forward. Evidently, he's quite confident I have this and now my confidence is up.

Suddenly, as sure as I was about this test I'm now getting nervous. The sweat collects on my head and brow as if there is a light rain in the car. I drive up to the testing line and a man signals for me to pull up to where he's standing in front of an orange cone.

"We're here," I say, waking Mr. Kay.

"Good job, Rick. I'll be right here when you're done. I know this clown. He's easy, don't worry." Mr. Kay grabs his Tums and eases out of the car.

The tester switches places with Mr. Kay, pulls on his seat belt, gets out his clip board and takes information off my permit. "Okay," he says. "You're going to turn out of the driveway, take a right and go to the first stop sign." His voice is robotic and his head doesn't move without his torso. It gets me thinking that maybe all the testers are robots and they're probably sending video feed back to the mainframe where some little guy is ticking off my every move. I fake sneeze to see if he'll say bless you, but he doesn't. He keeps his eyes forward and occasionally looks at my hands which are properly placed at the two and ten o'clock position. I don't dare talk, I follow his every command and by the end of the test I'm convinced he is indeed a robot.

I'm afraid to ask but I ask anyway. "Did I pass?"

"Flying colors," the tester drones.

I pull up to Mr. Kay and deliver the good news.

"That's great, Rick. How about a shake for old time's sake?" Mr. Kay moves his seat back and sets it in the reclining position. He eats two more Tums and closes his eyes.

Driving to Sonic Burger is the best drive I've ever done. I'm a licensed driver! Dad has a friend across town who told me he'd give me a job delivering wings once I got my license and that time is now! I'll be the best damn delivery guy there is.

I pull up and place an order for two shakes. I turn to give Mr. Kay his triple double chocolate shake and hold the freezing cold cup against his arm, thinking I'll jolt him awake. He doesn't move. In fact, his eyes are slightly open as is his mouth and I'm beginning to think Mr. Kay is dead. My heart pounds and I feel a blob in my throat like I swallowed a thousand cotton balls. I pull over to the curb, get out and go around to Mr. Kay's side. I open the door and gently shake his shoulder.

"Yo, Mr. Kay," I say.

No movement.

"Mr. Kay," I say louder this time.

Still nothing.

I've never had a need for a cell phone so I've never asked for one, but I sure could use one now. I check Mr. Kay's pocket for his phone and dial 9-1-1. How sick is this? Looking at Mr. Kay, I start thinking about how fat he is, *was*, I mean. Then I think, in a bunch of years this could be me. I vow right then and there that I will not be as fat as Mr. Kay when I'm old. I know deep down that I need to do *something*. I need to do something.

Mr. Kay looks like he's sleeping, not dead. It has to be a heart attack and maybe I should be doing something but I'm afraid to touch him. Maybe I should be giving him CPR? I check his wrist for a pulse and of course, there is none. This is so not cool. Where's Dr. Phil when you need him? Where's any doctor?

By the time the police, the fire department and the ambulance get to us, rigor mortis has set in and our shakes are melted. I explain to the cops that Mr. Kay is my Driver's Ed teacher and that he took me for my road test. I'm thinking here I get my license and Mr. Kay steals my celebratory moment. Then I feel like I should ground myself for thinking that very thought. I just know everyone at school will turn this into a big joke, like *I* killed Mr. Kay.

So much for going unnoticed.

FAT_vs_FICTION@BLOGSLOP.COM

Photos of me: 0

Profile: Round

Friends: 5

PAST BLOGS:

Find Cuisine

Big Beautiful

Save the Whales

Bananas

Glut vs. Guilt

Exorcist

Exorcist redux

No Sugar

Fire the Help

Last Man

Click here for more...

Sequestered

Haven't been able to blog in a couple of days. I've been sequestered. Yes, that's right folks. They got me.

I'm living in the happy hallowed halls of a fat farm. Okay, it's not really a fat farm 'cause there are all kinds of people here with eating disorders and some are pretty bony. I'm trying to think about how I got here and why my folks would put me in a place like this. It's not like I'm crazy. They think I'm "out of control". I think the hole in the wall and my being mean to the Russian was the last straw for them. Plus, the Russian found all that food hidden all over my room. Talk about thorough. Maybe Magda knew I was hiding stuff, but why didn't she tell?

So here I am with what I would consider a bunch of crazies. There are mostly people who won't eat. Why couldn't I be one of those people with anorexia or bulimia? Those bulimics have some brains. At least they eat. They just toss it when they're done. I say, why let all that food go to waste?

Is my eating a sickness? I think not. I'm neither anorexic or bulimic. What I have, I'm told, is a compulsive eating disorder. Yes, there's a name to why I'm so fat.

They're trying to tell me that this disorder is associated with one who no longer eats food for nutrition or enjoyment, but for emotional reasons like being happy or depressed. I supposedly have difficulty coping with my emotions and have low self-esteem. Like I need a doctor to tell me that!

So food is supposed to fill the void or help me escape from the feelings I don't want to deal with. I'm an addict. At least that's what they tell me.

I tell them that I still enjoy food. I'm not emotionally void when I'm eating. I'm happy when I'm eating. Food sends signals to my brain that there is love in my mouth. The taste and the feeling of being satisfied with every bite is my deal. I don't need to be in here.

Do I?

0 comments

Chapter 18

It's the Media Center and another round with the Einsteins before the Challenge. We really didn't need any more studying but Enid feels more secure if we're practicing, and nobody ever wants to disappoint Enid.

There are all these pamphlets from different colleges spread out over each and every table at the library. We've stumbled on College Career Day and the place is buzzing with Juniors and Seniors. I don't see The Oak at any of the tables. He's got scholarships locked in for playing football. The guy doesn't even have to work at it, or be smart, he just has to be who he is, a jock. Me, I've got to submit applications to all the schools, just like everyone else, even if I am smarter than most people. On grades alone, I could probably have my pick of the litter, but if I have to be interviewed, well, will prejudice reign 'cause I'm fat? I hear tell it that you can have two qualified candidates for one job and even if the fat guy is a little better at it, they go for the one with the presence. That's right. Looks count.

Enid picks up a pamphlet from Stanford, pushes her glasses closer to her eyes and smiles. "I am so going there. I could heal the world with labs like these. What about you, Rick? Where are you thinking of going?"

"Brown. Yale. Penn. I haven't made up my mind yet but I'm going Ivy. At least that should make my parents proud." I fan out the brochures on the table and choose The London School of Economics. "Might be nice to go far away, don't you think?"

"I'm staying in America," Max says. "No leaving this country. I like it too much."

Enid pushes the Stanford brochure at me. "Science. Think science. You're good at it, Rick. Brains like yours, we could heal the world together."

"Sounds like you're on a mission, Enid." I snort. "Why don't we just join the peace corps?"

"I'd do that." she says.

"I bet you would. Me, I think I'd have to pass. Too many shots for Malaria and all those other rainforest, deep jungle diseases. Besides, I'm not exactly the nature type. Live in a hut? Where's the video games, TV, and more importantly, the refrigerator?"

"Oh Rick, you're such an ass sometimes. You could have a chance at doing some good and all you can think of is electronics and appliances?" Enid rolls her eyes.

"I'll save the world in an air conditioned lab, thank you very much." I read about the Stanford science program until Kyle completes our foursome.

"Oh my God! I just met the cutest boy from Harvard and he is soooooooooooo gay. I am so going to Harvard. Smart and queer! It doesn't get any better than that. Doesn't get any better," he stammers. "Going to fill out my application right here."

"No you're not," Enid pulls the papers away from him. "We've got some studying to do. Let's get to it."

Challenge after challenge we realize we can't be beat. There's not a question one of us can't answer. The only problem is you never know who will be chosen for which question – it's a random process.

"Try and memorize every answer, even if it's not yours," Max takes over. "We have to be sure we can answer even the weakest of our subjects. Kyle, you brush up on the equations; Enid, you have everything down but a little more on the sonnets; Rick, I'm not worried about you. You just do your thing." Max smiles at me. "You're our ringer, but still, no guarantees they'll call on you."

"But we can confer, right?" Kyle asks.

"I believe they give you only thirty seconds to confer and then the chosen one has to answer. We can do it. I've got faith." Enid makes the sign of the cross.

"That's not the faith we need, Enid." Kyle says. He's anti-church since they're anti-gay. "We need faith in our team."

"That, we've got," I say, making sure to smile at each and every one of our team. "We have each other and I don't think anyone can measure up to our incredible minds!"

I put my hand in the middle of the table waiting for the cliché moment that everyone will pile their hands on mine and break with a big old *booyah*! I guess Dylan is rubbing off on me a little.

"One for all!" I take another brochure off the table and they haven't even got a clue of what I was trying to do. We're just a bunch of socially inept geniuses. How sad.

Walking Enid home we get to talking about Mr. Kay and the fact that he died on my watch.

"Didn't you notice anything? Was he clutching his heart or was he quietly in agony?" Enid is genuinely concerned. "He was such a nice man."

"The best. He was like, my friend, almost. And no,

there was no big drama at all. One minute he's eating Tums, takes me to my driving test, and the next minute he's sleeping – or so I thought." I raise an eyebrow, like how can I not notice something, smart as I am.

"Nothing? Wow. I hope I go like that. No drama, just quietly fade." Enid picks up a small stone and puts it in her pocket.

"You collect those?" Should I have asked that question? Maybe it's like a compulsive disorder, I just seem to say stupid things, or observational things out loud.

"What?"

"Stones. You're always finding stones and putting them in your pocket." Deep, huh?

"I collect things I like. I have lots of collections of small things. Pebbles are pretty. I collect stamps, but I don't put them in an album. I collect miniatures but I don't have a doll house. I don't know, I like *things*."

"What's your favorite thing that you collect?" We're standing in Enid's driveway now. Maybe next time I'll borrow Dad's car and be able to drive her home. Maybe next time we'll talk in my car.

"I have a collection of these little plastic charms, animal charms that used to be my mom's. She loved it whenever she would go to a store and her mom would give her a penny to put in those gum machines, only she collected those little plastic animals. I have an entire circus!" Enid smiles the biggest smile. Something makes her really happy.

What something makes me that happy?

Walking home I think about it. I think about my own happiness and what my passions are. I think about what I really want to do with my life once College starts and way after that when school is over. Do I want to teach? Do I want to just lie around watching episodes of Oprah and Dr. Phil? Do I want to become a forensics guy so I can dispel myths and nab the bad guy? I like forensics. I like the sound of it, too. I'm in forensics. Hey, don't touch the crime scene until the forensics guy gets here. Way important. Science and criminology, the perfect mix. I probably know a lot of stuff just from all those shows I watch. And who knows? Maybe I'll come up with a way to have DNA in a day.

FAT_vs_FICTION@BLOGSLOP.COM

Photos of me: 0

Profile: Round

Friends: 5

PAST BLOGS:

Big Beautiful

Save the
Whales

Bananas

Glut vs. Guilt

Exorcist

Exorcist redux

No Sugar

Fire the Help

Last Man

Sequestered

*Click here
for more...*

Blame

Yup. You heard it here. They say your parents are partly to blame. Partly is me being nice. Maybe they're ALL to blame.

When I was little, if I was upset, my grandmother would give me a cookie. That, my friends, if I have any left out there, is the story of my life. They don't call it comfort food for nothing.

So here's the skinny (sic) of it all: A kid cries, mom or dad gives the kid a piece of candy to make them happy, and the kid can't develop any "coping mechanisms". Yes, that's the whole scoop and nothing but the scoop. So, I, they tell me, learned to associate food with emotions. And it's a vicious cycle 'cause you eat to be happy, then feel guilty for eating, gain weight and feel guilty for gaining weight and then we feel guilty for feeling guilty. So we eat to compensate for all that guilt. You follow me?

Then come the barrage of diets. I don't know about you, but like I said before, I've tried them all. We're in this "group" of kids who don't want to talk and the shrink is doing all the talking. She's asking us if we feel "good enough" being who we are? Do we feel good about anything other than food? Or in the bony girl's problem, why doesn't food make her feel good?

I think they shouldn't lump us together. I think we need to separate the fat kids from the skinny ones. It's not fair. They're talking about how food disgusts them and I'm like, are you crazy! Oh yeah, that's why we're here.

There are these two girls here that are "chewers". Get this. They chew their food for the flavor and they think for the vitamins, and spit the food out. What's the point? I say let them eat cake and swallow it!

Okay, so they're trying to tell us how this cycle of dieting and binge eating can go on forever unless the emotional attachment or detachment to food is broken. What emotional attachment? I just don't get it.

Not like I'm in love with my Twinkie...

992 comments

Life is kind of like a sinking ship and who wants a fat kid onboard? Sorry about your woes Dude. Sounds like you need a friend.

Chapter 19

"Dude, wake up."

It's Dylan. "Wake up. It's polar time."

"Go away." I lift my head, a string of drool pulling from my pillow. "I'm not going with you."

Dylan pulls the quilt off my no longer warm body and pulls at my shirt. "Let's go, Bud."

"Alright, alright, but I'm hanging in the car." I move at a snail's pace and search for my jeans in the dark. It's midnight and I may have only had a half an hour of sleep before Dylan came to shake me out of my dreams.

"No problem, my man. But first, where do your folks keep their liquor?"

"Liquor? Are you insane? It's a school night and uh, we're not old enough to drink."

"Just to keep us warm." Dylan does not sound reassuring.

I can hear my Grandma Irene now. Be careful what you wish for, she would always say. But how careful can you be if your only wish is for a double bacon cheeseburger smothered in onions and ketchup?

Be careful what you wish for. Now I'm standing at a lake in Woodland Park with Dylan, The Oak and all the Jockstraps, who on Perry's dare are going to go polar skinny dipping. God, I hope they don't think I'm any part of this. The weather has been getting colder since Halloween, colder than I can remember and here they are stripping down to their bare asses.

I watch them jump into the water on Perry's command. Like a bunch of synchronized swimmers they all take the plunge.

"C'mon in, Rick, the water's fine," The Oak yells.

"Leave him alone, Oak." Dylan, my self-proclaimed protector tries to keep the Oak in his place.

The thing of it is, I wish I could strip down to nothing, jump in the water and act like a total goofball. Truth of it is, I'm not about to play sumo wrestler, dive into the lake and set off a tsunami. Nope, can't do it.

I look at the bottle of alcohol at my feet. Bourbon. Of all the things Dylan could have robbed from my parent's bar, it was bourbon. Not that I was planning on drinking, but any normal kid might have taken the vodka, or beer even. Not Dylan.

"This shit'll warm you good, right to the soul. Besides," Dylan raised a sinister eyebrow, "nobody else will want to drink it. More for us."

"Us?" I do not and do not plan on letting that vile crap near my gullet. "Dude, I don't drink."

"Never? I mean, you've never gotten drunk?

I wasn't sure whether to be embarrassed or proud. Why would I ever have had an occasion to drink, let alone get drunk? I know that there was never an opportunity for me to have gotten drunk until now. Still, I have to stay in control. I'm driving now.

Perry Parker is calling them all ladies. He thought up this dare with the help of something he read on the internet about hazing and according to Dylan, the idea got under his skin and he wouldn't let up until the guys agreed to do it. By the time they got drunk enough to jump into the lake it was close to two a.m. Now it's near three and they're still horsing around. How none of them are showing signs of hypothermia is a mystery.

I stumble back into the trees hoping the surrounding leaves will warm me. I wish I kept my coat of many words, the one I wanted to burn but threw in the trash instead. I think of going back to the car but then Dylan will think I left. The wind is kicking up and I hear voices coming closer.

"Rick, you there?" Dylan's teeth chatter off in the distance. "Dude?"

I'm about to answer when I realize the voices are The Oak's and Perry Parker. At least they had the good sense to step out of the lake to piss.

"It's freakin' freezing!" The Oak says, peeing on a bush.

"Dude, that's my foot, you moron!" Perry pushes The Oak.

"I'm drunk. Sorry, bad aim." The Oak laughs.

I'm listening to this little pishap and it's obvious they don't know I'm here, probably forgot I even came with Dylan.

Perry grabs a sweatshirt from a pile of clothes and wraps it around his waste. "Man, let's take their clothes and ditch 'em." Perry laughs.

They sort through the pile and leave only their stuff on the ground. Perry pushes the clothes at The Oak and they head out for the woods. I have to see this. I follow them but stay back more than a few feet and even though it's dark, I try to keep to the even darker shadows of the trees.

"Hear that?" The Oak whispers.

It's the snapping of twigs under my feet. The trees have begun to lose their leaves and nobody rakes up the woods. I try to be sleuth-like but it's nearly impossible to be quiet. My feet sink into muddy piles of leaves.

Perry stops to listen. I stop and wait, my breath heavy in the night.

The Oak drops a pair of jeans on the ground and doesn't move to pick them up.

"Probably just a squirrel or something." Perry says. "C'mon, grab that and let's go."

All this time I thought Oak called the shots. Now I'm thinking Perry is the force behind the Jockstraps. Perry is the one Dylan needs to watch out for.

"What if there are snakes?" The Oak says.

Snakes? I didn't think about the wildlife out here. I'm more an asphalt kind of guy. I get grossed out when it rains and worms are crawling along the cracks on sidewalks. Snakes? Who am I kidding? I can't follow these guys any further. I turn to go back but then I hear Perry shoot off some more commands.

"Dump them here," he says.

The Oak starts laughing so loud Perry has to cover his mouth with one of the T-shirts.

"You want them to find their stuff? Shut up, you idiot!"

Now I'm sure I'm hallucinating. Did I just hear Perry call The Oak an idiot? All this time I've had it so wrong. Wait until I tell Dylan.

I wait while The Oak and Perry head back and don't move until I hear them jump into the lake. One of the Jockstraps comments on how long it takes to pee when you're cold. Brains are not their strong suit. I grab the pile of clothes and make my way back to the lake, placing them right back where they were before the guys got to them.

If I really was one of the guys, wouldn't I horse around, too? Now I've got The Oak's Jeans and Perry's Khakis. I head for another spot in the woods. This time, no snake is going to stop me from pulling the ultimate prank.

Back at the lake I sit in clear view with the bottle of Bourbon. I'm pretty much invisible and nobody is riding me, nobody bothering me at all. I think about Mr. Kay and how he was one of my only real friends. Rolling the bottle of Bourbon in my hand, I twist off the cap and ready my lips for whatever comes their way. I take one sip and hold it in my mouth just a little too long. My tongue is on fire and I immediately feel like barfing. Instead of swallowing, I turn my head and spit so the guys don't see me.

Drinking. Not my style.

***

"Let's get out," a Jockstrap yells. "I'm turning blue."

"How can you tell in the dark, you moron," Perry yells back.

"I'm out of here," I hear Dylan say.

I watch as they climb out of the lake and head for their clothes. I watch even closer for The Oak and Perry's reaction. They look at each other and bend to get their stuff out of the pile.

It's like slapstick watching the other guys try to dress in their jeans while their bodies are wet and apparently a little drunk. Dylan practically falls while pulling on his sweats, stumbles over and grabs the bottle of bourbon. I'm still watching The Oak and Perry who, dressed only in a shirt and sweatshirt, make a b-line for me.

"Nice ass!" one of the Jockstraps yells and the others let out a few cat calls.

"What did you do with our clothes, Dickhead?" Perry pulls me up on my feet, which I'm pretty impressed he can do as drunk as he is. He and the Oak both don't have any pants on and I have to do everything I can not to laugh. I'm thinking I should be really scared about now, but I'm not.

Dylan takes a swig of bourbon, looks at them and bursts out laughing. "What the hell are you guys doing?"

"Our clothes?" The Oak moves in and demands, his breath hot on my face.

"Move it." I push him away. "I don't know what you're talking about."

"It had to be him," Perry says to The Oak. "Who else was out here while we were in the lake?"

I don't know what comes over me but I feel like I have nothing to lose. I know I'm putting myself out there but I'm going to do it anyway. "Must have been a squirrel!" I laugh. I think twice about the shrinkage comment I'm about to let loose when Perry's fist meets my stomach. Although I've got all this cushioning going on, I feel it. I feel dinner rising from my gut, take a deep breath through my nose and realize I'm still standing. I get down on my knees and Dylan is just sitting there, as if he's totally numb.

"I thought you could take these guys," I whisper. What happened to breaking the Oak's limbs? Where's that guy?

Dylan doesn't say two words, nor does he come to my side like the true fighter I thought he was.

"Now, Rick, where are they?" The Oak is down on one knee and in my face again.

"Where's what?" I ask innocently. This sudden burst of bravery is so not me. I see Perry about to give me another taste of his big bad self and spill the beans. "The woods, just a little further than where you dumped their clothes," I give in. I'm not cut out for pranks and consequences. Truth is, there was a bit of a thrill in thinking I could pull it off, but really, who am I kidding?

"Go get them." The Oak commands.

I adjust my eyes to the darkness and retrace my steps through the woods and over to their pants. My stomach still hurts a little but what the heck, it was an iota of fun in my otherwise miniscule social life. Back at the lake, I hand over their pants and back away.

"Consider that your initiation, asswipe." Perry yells over his shoulder.

Initiation? I look at Dylan who is now sprawled on his back humming to the stars, totally oblivious to anything around him. I think drinking isn't his thing either.

"C'mon, Dylan. Time to go home." I get up first and pull him to his feet. The bottle is affixed to his hand and I pry his fingers off the neck. "You're done with this," I say, spilling the remaining bourbon out.

"Sorry, man." Dylan whispers.

"About what? Not coming to my rescue when I was being pounded by Perry Parker? Oh, that was nothing. I can take it." And I did, too. But, that didn't make it any easier. I'm thinking, sorry isn't enough. "Why didn't you help me out back there?"

"You have to man up, Dude. What do you think –"

Dylan stumbles, almost falling on me. His face is an inch from mine, his breath smelling like he drank the lake instead of swimming in it. "You think I'm here to protect you, like some big brother or something. That's not for me."

"I didn't ask you to fight my battles. A little help would have been nice. Or maybe, let's say, asking those guys to back off!" I'm looking Dylan right in the eyes but he avoids mine. I was starting to think we *were* like brothers. "You're just like them Dylan. You're no better than they are! A bunch of empty-headed asinine jockstraps."

"Oh, yeah," Dylan yells. "When I'm with those empty-headed asinine jockstraps, I'm home." Dylan runs his fingers through his hair, stands up as straight as he can and heads for the car. "This is bullshit. Let's just go home, Rick. I'm done."

"Yeah, me too." I say, only I'm not. I don't want Dylan mad at me. Heck, I'm the one that should be angry, but that's not my M.O. Guess I'm a lot like Mom in that sense. I don't have that hold-a-grudge gene. "I get it, Dylan. And, sorry about all this."

Dylan sighs and forces a smile. "No problem, it's all part of the project."

The project? If there was a grade involved, I'd so get an F.

FAT_vs_FICTION@BLOGSLOP.COM

Photos of me: 0

Profile: Round

Friends: 5

PAST BLOGS:

BBW

Whales

Bananas

Glut

Exorcism

Exorcism 2

No sugar

Fire the help!

Last man

Sequestered

Parents

*Click here
for more...*

I don't buy it

Today's discussion is dedicated to us compulsive eaters. The anorexics are disgusted by even the mere mention of food. The compulsive eaters are drooling.

Eating is not a disease that I can take a pill for and cure. It's not something we can even cure with a diet, lose weight and be okay for the rest of our lives. The doc is saying that diets actually do more damage to people like me. She says compulsive eating is incurable and serious and to remember IT IS NOT MY FAULT I'm fat.

I did not cause this. I can not cure it. But arming myself with how I got here and why I eat will enable me to live a happy, joyous and wonderful life. More than I ever dreamed possible.

Do you buy that? I sure don't. It's bullshit.

First of all, if there's one thing my Dad always told me it's to be responsible for who I am today. It's my fault I eat. It's my fault I'm fat. I have choices and I choose not to fix it. Or at least I chose not to fix it in the past.

I take a little of what they say and make it my own. But I sure as hell don't buy into all of it.

My days here are tutoring in the morning, followed by afternoon walks, and then group. I don't think I'll be here too long but they want to follow my life patterns and "assess" where changes can be made.

I will say this, I'm hungrier than ever. They've got me on like 2,000 calories a day and all the sugar free jello I can eat. There are no vending machines but I can usually swipe a piece of cake from the bony girls and then it looks like they're eating. But that doesn't happen too often. There are eyes everywhere.

As much as I hate it here, I worry about home. Who is going to watch me there? The Russian spy? Mom and Dad are due here for a family meeting. That is some-thing I'm not looking forward to. Mom will blame Dad, Dad will blame me, I'll blame the aliens. Blah, blah, blah.

60 comments

Definitely, blame the aliens. Have you been probed yet?

Chapter 20

Dylan's out not home and that suits me fine. I've forgotten how it is to be an only child, being ignored in the house and, in retrospect, not minding it too much. Now I'm back at the computer, surfing diets, like old times.

In the search bar, I type in: *How to win the battle of the bulge?* There's the cabbage diet, grapefruit diet, a diet for making your stomach flatter and a Jesus diet. No kidding, just *Google* it! Oh, and there's a diet of breathing air and taking your body to a higher realm. Uh, I think that's called death. Who are they kidding?

Ultimately it comes to the same thing again and again. No miracles. Slow and steady wins the race. I never won a race in my life. I pull out the *post-it* I have under my desk and with Mom's credit card info on it and sign up for Weight Watchers online program. This way I don't have to see anyone. I reluctantly put in my starting weight and wait for the computer to blow up. It doesn't. Instead, I am welcomed into a community of people like me, somewhat desperate, somewhat depressed and maybe, somewhat relieved.

I read over the plans and am encouraged to choose the right one for me. The right one for me would be one that includes cake and ice cream and get this, there is one! I will start tomorrow. Tomorrow is the best day of the week, and since I have half a day left I am going to enjoy every morsel that touches these lips.

The guy in the blog I read, *Fat vs. Fiction*, he's in real trouble, all because he likes to eat. His parents locked him up in some nut house or place for foodaholics and I'm thinking I better do something before someone sends me away.

I'm about to get ready for the final meet of the Einsteins before the challenge, when Mom comes down the stairs with the phone in one hand and Aunt Diane's ashes in the other.

"What are you doing with that now?" I ask, pointing to the urn.

"I'm just not sure where she'll be happiest," Mom looks around the room. Does she not see the billions of boxes?

"Oh, this is for you," Mom says, handing me the phone.

"Where's Dylan?" I ask, covering the phone. I worry that he'll see Mom doing this again.

"Out for his run," she says absentmindedly.

I watch her wander around my lair, give up and walk

back up the stairs with Aunt Diane. Nothing against Aunt Diane, but having her ashes down here would give me the creeps. Bad enough she's been sitting in the formal living room. We don't go in there as it is and now it's been converted into a mausoleum. I shiver every time I pass that room. Don't know how Dylan can stand it knowing his dead mother's ashes are in the house.

"Hello?" I almost forgot about the phone.

"Hey, Rick? It's Enid."

I can barely hear her. "Enid? Can you speak a little louder?"

"No, I'm at the library," she whispers.

"Okay," I automatically whisper back.

"Can we come to your house to study? There's something going on at the library and there's no place for us to talk."

"Uh, I guess so. How long?" My palms are starting to sweat. I don't think I've ever had friends over, even if they are only the Einsteins.

"Now. Ten minutes?" Enid says.

"Alrighty then, See you in ten."

I hang up the phone and start to freak. Should I have them down here? I look at the big groove for my ass on the couch and think it will be better to have them upstairs at the dining room table. I take the stairs two at a time and think I'm about to pass out when I reach the top.

"Rick, what is it? Are you okay?" Mom rushes to my side.

"Einsteins…coming…now."

"What Rick? You're not making any sense." Mom pulls me toward her. "Are you sick?"

"No, Mom." I catch my breath. "The Einsteins are coming here to study for our challenge. The competition is next week. Remember?"

"How can I forget my number one son." Mom starts picking up around the house. "How about the dining room table?"

"That's what I thought." I go and get some pads and pencils from Mom's Bunco game and set up the table.

"Snacks," Mom says placing a bowl of chips on the table. "Sodas?"

"Sure, Mom. Thanks."

***

We have one week left to really kick some ass and this is the last time we will get together before the Challenge. I'm ready, we all are, but we need each other to feel real, to feed off each other somehow.

Enid passes out index cards with problems written on them. We write our name on a few pieces of paper, fold them up and throw them into one of Mom's bowls. That's how random it will be at the Challenge and we need to be ready.

I choose Enid's name and give her the first question.

"You are on a game show. The host shows you ten doors. He says one door has ten million dollars behind it, the other nine doors have nothing. You must choose a door. Oooooh, the suspense!" My eyebrows dance on my forehead sinisterly.

"Okay, so I choose my door. It will have to be random because how can you deduce anything from ten closed doors?" Enid pushes her aviators onto the bridge of her nose.

"Random it is. Now, the host says, "Let's see how you did?" He opens the door you picked."

"Did I choose correctly?" Enid asks, the corners of her mouth turning up ever so slightly.

"What? It can't be that easy. There's more." Kyle urges. "Let the man finish!"

"Okay, so he keeps your door shut and opens another door...nothing. He opens another and still nothing. He continues to open doors until there are only two doors left, the door you chose and one other door. Got that so far?"

"Yes, so she's no closer to the money than I was when I

chose the first door." Max says. "This is like that *Deal or No Deal* game which the masses watch."

I grab a couple of chips and cram them into my mouth. Everyone waits until I'm done chewing to finish the question. "Now, the host says 'the prize is behind one of these two doors. You can stay with your door, or switch to the other door.' Should you stay or switch doors? Why? What is the probability of winning for each door?"

Kyle jumps in. "Obvious! It's a fifty-fifty probability."

"No," Enid explains. "When I chose the door in the first place I had a one in ten chance of getting it. The other door is the answer. You should switch because the other door has nine-tenths probability of having the money, which makes your odds better."

Max scratches his head and sighs. "I hope they don't ask this one. I hate game shows."

The front door slams and Dylan comes in, body glistening of sweat from his run. He throws his towel on the stairs and kicks off his sneakers at the front door. Kyle's head spins so fast I think it's going to snap off.

"Hey," Dylan salutes the group on his way to the kitchen.

"Who is that?" Kyle perks right up. "I've seen him around school."

"That, Kyle, is my *straight* cousin, Dylan." I know how Dylan feels about the opposite sex but I don't really know where he stands on boy-meets-boy. "Cool it, Kyle."

"I'm cool, I'm cool." Kyle straightens up in his seat. "You never know, there's someone for everyone." Kyle points to Dylan. "Even *he* could like me."

"Yeah, right," I snort. "Kyle, unless you've got a magic wand…"

"Maybe I do." Kyle says defiantly.

"Even so, it's hopeless." I state very clearly.

"What's that supposed to mean?" Enid asks.

"That, dear Enid, means that there is no way Dylan is for Kyle here, and there is no way that there is someone for me." I cross my arms and block myself from the universe.

"That's ridiculous!" She pounds a fist on the table. "There *is* someone for everyone."

"Okay," I challenge. "You're going to tell me that someone could look at me and say, wow!" I smack myself in the forehead, "that's the guy for me!"

"Well, perhaps once they've gotten to know you," Enid says quietly.

"Exactly! That's just my point. Nobody gives you a chance to see what's *inside,* they can't get past the flesh. Nobody wants to know you if you're –"

"What? German?" Max laughs. We all do.

"German, fat, gay, geeky, what's the difference?" Enid says. "We've all got some particular *thing* about us, everyone does."

"Not everyone," I say. "What about the Jockstraps, what about the RahRahs, what about the foreign exchange students? They've all got the world by the balls." I look to Enid to make sure I haven't offended her. I don't think I have, so I continue. "They have these perfect worlds and we don't fit in."

"I fit," Enid says quietly.

"I fit," Kyle echoes.

Max and I don't join in their reindeer games. I'm thinking about what to say next when Dylan comes out and hands me the phone.

"Yes, this is Rick. Oh, hello. How are you? I'm sorry about...yes, well...I'll have to ask my parents...but, really? He said that? Um, sure, hold on please."

I look at the phone and then scream for Mom to pick it up. When I hear her voice, I hang up the receiver and stare at the Einsteins.

"That was Mrs. Kay, you know, the driver's ed teacher's wife. She wants to *give* me his car. Says Mr. Kay always talked about me, says he was talking about offering to sell me the car if I would take it. Says he was going to retire next year anyway and now she wants to *give* it to me."

"That's no car," says Kyle. "That's a boat!"

"Gas is going to cost you a fortune," Max adds.

"Fortune? I just got a car, for free! That in itself is worth the inflated price of gas." I pace around the table. Enid's head follows my every move. "I have wheels! I'm mobile. I can get a job. I can drive!"

"Good," Enid says. "Now you can drive us all to the Challenge together."

"You, my fellow Einstein, have a deal," I say. "And I have a car."

I feel bad for Mr. Kay, feel bad that he died of a heart attack, feel bad that he died in *that* car, but the thought of having my own wheels is way beyond cool. I take a minute to breathe and hope the probability of Mom saying yes is one hundred percent.

FAT_vs_FICTION@BLOGSLOP.COM

You are what you eat

I'm like a banana. Peel off the thick, slightly bruised skin and inside I'm just mush.

Someone, please get me out of this place.

Photos of me: 0

Profile: Round

Friends: 5

My folks showed up and it was exactly how I thought it would be. It went something like this:

Doc: Want to share with your parents all the things you've been feeling while you've been here?

Me: Not particularly.

PAST BLOGS:

Save the Whales

Bananas

Glut vs. Guilt

Exorcist

Exorcist redux

No Sugar

Fire the Help

Last Man

Sequestered

Blame

Click here for more...

Mom: Talk to us baby, tell us what you're feeling. The sooner you do, the sooner you'll be better and we can bring you home.

Me: I'm not going to get "better" 'cause I'm not sick. Maybe it's the two of you who are sick. Have you ever thought of that? Who put me here in the first place, jerks!

Dad: Don't talk to us that way. It's your fault (Dad says to my mom), always feeding him dessert after every meal. That's not how I was raised. That was all your doing.

Mom: Don't go blaming me for this. You are as much to blame.

Doc: This isn't about blaming anyone. Please, we need to come together and work toward helping your son deal with why he eats, how to deal with his own emotions better. We need to work toward building his self esteem.

Mom: What's wrong with his self-esteem.

Dad: (slaps forehead.)

Me: (I leave the room.)

146 comments

I'll bake you a cake with a file, dude. You can escape.

Chapter 21

Mr. Searcy, my Dad's friend and infamous owner of Wright Wings, is as blunt as he is a Republican. Dad calls him a no bullshit man and I am learning first hand, why.

"Rick, son, I'm going to start you as a driver. If I put you up at the register, what message would that send?" Mr. Searcy sets a stack of not-so-earth-friendly takeout boxes on the counter.

"Message?" All I want to do is drive. I don't want to be a cashier.

"You know, message." He does the air quote thing. "If someone comes in and sees a boy of your, well, girth, what message does that send? Wings make you fat?"

I'm speechless.

"Of course wings make you fat. Everything in this

place will make you fat, but we don't want to ram it down their throats, right? So, I say to myself, if you're delivering, they're looking at the food and their money, not at you." Mr. Searcy pats my shoulder. "Put this shirt on and you're ready to work. If it doesn't fit, I'll order you a bigger one."

I hold up the light blue tee which is covered in clouds, a runway, and a cartoon of Wilbur and Orville Wright on the front. By the time I pull the not-so-extra-large shirt over my head, Wilbur and Orville have taken flight. I look ridiculous. To top it off, Searcy hands me a hat with foamy silver wings on each side of my head.

"You're kidding, right?" I look at Mr. Searcy, hat in my hand.

"Nope...you're a Wing Man now, son. Get out there and show us what you've got."

I've got a big ass Buick, thanks to my dead driver's ed teacher and a shirt that's hugging me so tight my armpits are aching, and there's no way on earth I'm putting this thing on my head. I grab the first two orders, set the GPS Mr. Searcy gave me to the first address and drive off down Water Street. It's weird driving Mr. Kay's car around. I can't even call it mine. It will always be Mr. Kay's. Mom and Dad agreed it would be a great starter car. The thing is built like a tank and if I get into an accident, at least my precious body will be protected. I don't think they made air bags back then but the fat around my bones should protect me plenty. Mr. Kay had to get seat belt extenders when I started taking lessons. At least I have those.

"Thanks, Mr. Kay," I say out loud. Then I think, what if he's haunting me? What if this car and driver's ed is something he loved so much that he's going to sit beside me forever? I've really gotta stop watching those horror movies with Dad. I slowly crane my neck to check out the passenger seat, ready to see the ghost of Mr. Kay, when the GPS talks and scares the spit right out of me!

"Turn left in five hundred yards...." my GPS guide warns. She definitely sounds sure of where she's taking me.

"Turn left in two hundred yards." The smell of wings in garlic sauce overwhelm my senses. My mouth waters with every breath. I'm hungry.

"Recalculating route," I guess I got that wrong. "Make a U-turn at the first available point. Then turn right."

My stomach starts to rumble and I'm thinking I should have had snacks before working. I move the bags closer to get a better whiff. I'm thinking that they might not miss one wing, right? I'm thinking they'll be snarfing down their wings so fast, they won't know something's missing. To even it out, I take a wing from both boxes and slowly nibble off the skin, the flesh, and toss the bones out the window. The only witness is the voice on the GPS and I don't think she'll be scolding me anytime soon. My fingers are sticky with sauce and I think I might start keeping my own bottle of hot sauce and napkins in the glove compartment.

I find the house for my very first delivery and pray they don't call my boss, complaining that they've been short changed two wings. Now all I can think of is an order of drumettes and curly fries.

"Where's the hat?" a little kid asks when he opens the door.

"What hat? Is your mom home?" The scent of the wings grow stronger.

"The funny hat with the wings. Can you put it on?" The kid points to my ears.

"I left it home."

The kid starts whining to his mother that I don't have the hat on and she eyes me like it's my fault the kid is going to cry. Okay, okay, I'll go get the hat. I hand the woman the food and the bill.

"I'll get it." I say it begrudgingly, but I go get it.

I come back to the door with the hat on and the kid is happy.

"Bend down," he commands.

Stooping to his level is not an easy feat for a fat guy, but I get down on one knee and he starts flapping my wings. How long do I have to put up with this, I wonder. What's the etiquette on saying goodbye and does my tip depend on it?

"Here you go. Keep the change." The woman gives me a twenty and hands the kid the bag. "Take this to the table," she tells him. "And thank you. That's one of the reasons I order from Wright Wings." She smiles and closes the door, leaving me with a three dollar tip and the scent of garlic.

I take out my cell phone, call Wright Wings, disguise my voice, give a bogus address, and order a tub of wings, extra hot. I'll eat them in my car while I deliver food to hungry people with little obnoxious kids who want to play with my wings.

Whatever. It's a job.

Just when I'm starting to relax again, I find out I have to deliver three tubs of wings, a couple pounds of curly fries and onion rings to the Sapperstein residence. Unless Candy has a very large, hungry family, there's a party going on. If there's a party going on you can be sure the Jockstraps will be there. I'm at the point where they tolerate me since the night at the lake. Being Dylan's cousin holds some weight, but if I show up in a shirt that's two sizes too small for me, I'm sure it will be social suicide.

There's no place to park and I can't double park or I'll block the road. I wind up having to park half way down the block. The doorbell at Candy's house sets off chimes like church bells, only these are the Sapperstein's. Candy's Bat Mitzvah was featured on the reality show, *Party Moms*, and it was the most talked about show at school for months. Cameras followed Candy and her mother's every step while they planned and preened for the party of the century.

I ring the bell a second time and The Oak answers the door, looks at me and yells over his shoulder, "Hey, Dylan, I didn't know your cousin was a delivery guy. He's got free food!"

"Not *free*, Oak." I'm reluctant to hand over the food.

"Free food!" a chorus comes from somewhere inside the house.

"Yeah, that's right. Rick here is buying us wings. Woohoo!" The Oak grabs the bag and shuts the door in my face. At first I'm dumbstruck, like what just happened? Then I realize I'm in a heaping pile of shit if I don't go back to Wright Wings with a fist full of cash for this order. I ring the bell and nobody comes to the door.

Here's what gets me more than anything, Dylan is inside and once again he's not doing anything about it. He's so become one of them. My blood is about to boil. I'm *not* leaving. I'm not making any more deliveries until I have my money. "Dylan!" I scream as loud as I can. I ring the bell again and Dylan comes to the door.

"Dude, don't make this worse than it already is," he whispers.

"Worse? My first night on the job, I'm not going back there Dylan without the money. You have to get me that money." I actually feel like I'm going to cry, but I hold back on the watershed.

"Look, go home, get some money and pay for it. I'll get your money back from them."

"What gives them the right, Dylan? Who do they think they are?" My voice cracks under pressure.

"They're the guys trying to get back at you for ditching their clothes, that's who they are. Now go away and I'll get your money by the end of the night. Mr. and Mrs. Sapperstein are the ones who offered up food, I'm sure they mean to pay. I'll take care of it." Dylan closes the door half way. "Now go."

Was I supposed to *man up* just then? I feel like a puppy with my tail between my legs, being sent away after doing something wrong, but it wasn't just me playing pranks at the lake. They were going to ditch everyone else's clothes, and that makes it okay? I just did all the other guys a favor. I did get their clothes back...eventually. I admit I loved the look on

Perry and The Oak's faces when they realized the guys clothes were all there, but not their own pants. Anyway, we all had a good laugh, except for Perry and The Oak. I was just doing what *any one of the guys* would do. I was just trying to be like them.

Dylan. He said he felt like he was home when he was with them. I do get it. I'm not a complete idiot, but letting them do this to me is so not cool. It's downright cruel. He could step in, do what's right, but hey, I've seen Dylan's loyalty waver before. Sure, he says he'll get the money, but there's no guarantee. Now I'm out the cash for the wings I ate and the money for the Sapperstein order.

Maybe Mr. Searcy will let me be the cook, or the guy who coats the wings with that hot sauce. I could do that job, make minimum wage and forget this stupid shirt and hat.

FAT_vs_FICTION@BLOGSLOP.COM

Photos of me: 0

Profile: Round

Friends: 5

PAST BLOGS:

Bananas

Glut vs. Guilt

Exorcist

Exorcist redux

No Sugar

Fire the Help

Last Man

Sequestered

Blame

You Are
What You Eat

*Click here
for more...*

Emotional Rescue

Breakthrough. That's what one of the bony girls had, an emotional rescue. She confessed to all of her sins. Not only is she a mess with the eating thing but she's a cutter.

I swear, I feel like I've been living inside a bottle with one of those ships, I'm so out of touch. I never get close enough to anyone to know that they have issues, big issues. I start thinking about all the people at school, the ones who are such assholes to me and I think about their lives.

I think if it makes them feel so good to make me feel so bad, there's got to be some deep emotional shit going on inside their own lives. Maybe they've got parents who belittle them. Maybe they've got an older brother or sister who is better than they are at everything and their parents favor the sibling. Or maybe they're just born jerks and they can't help themselves.

In any case, Doc says it's not about us, it's about them. If they need to make us feel bad, we have to fight that feeling. We have to fight back by holding our heads up and not letting them into our psyche, not let them under our skin. We have to grow some teflon balls.

It's not just kids though, it's parents too. Bad parenting. They might not realize the depth of the comments they make. They might not know that they're little snide remarks can hurt. It's abuse in one way or another. I don't really feel abused, but I know that my folks say stuff that definitely makes me feel like crap. And what do I do about it? Nothing.

Next time they come for family counseling I'm going to tell them just how much they hurt when they say things. I'm going to tell them the eating is my way of dealing with how much they fight. I'm going to ask them to stop and I'm going to ask for their help. I guess they were helping me by putting me in here.

I didn't think so at the time.

212 comments

Amen brother.

Chapter 22

"Here." Dylan hands me a wad of cash. "I got the money from the Sapersteins. Look, the guys were just punking you, they planned on paying you back all along."

"Punking?"

"Yeah, like I told you, it was to get back at you for hiding their clothes at the lake." Dylan laughs.

"It's not that funny." I'm certainly over it.

To make up for it, Dylan decides to ride with me while I make deliveries. After all this time I'm still not entirely sure of Dylan. I can't explain it but I just don't know who he'll be fifteen minutes from now. It's like, one minute I'm his "project", sometimes he's a friend, and other times I'm just his cousin who has become more like a shadow when those guys are around. With Dylan, you have to take each play one at a time.

Dylan waits in the car while I pick up a few orders. I show him how to plug an address into the GPS and he becomes copilot while we ride. Fortunately, no deliveries go to anyone I know and the night is pretty calm. I get us a couple of orders of wings which we snarf down with a couple orders of fries and onion rings. I'm getting pretty good at driving with one hand on the wheel and one on a drumstick.

"Hand me that Pepsi," I ask Dylan.

"Try this." He hands me celery with white stuff on it. They throw it in with every order or wings and I keep forgetting to tell them to hold the veggies.

"Nope. Don't do green." I stand by my words.

"Try it. It's not bad, really." Dylan shoves the celery in my mouth and I would toss it except I'm turning the car onto Botero Lane and need both hands. I crunch down on the celery and at first I'm not sure about the stringy texture, but then I get to this flavor burst and it's not too bad.

"See," Dylan says victoriously. "Green is not bad for you. Green is your friend! Maybe I'll get you to eat a salad someday."

"Maybe I'm ready to try," I say just above a whisper.

That guy that I've been reading about, the one with the blogs, he's still locked up. It's like being in jail just because you like food, a lot. Then I think about the fact that I'm in my own jail, this body of mine. I take another stick of celery, crunch it up and think this could be the first step to really making a change. I could start walking the track again and use the Torture-o-Matic. Does The Oak eat celery, I wonder?

"So how's it going for you?" I ask Dylan when I'm back in the car. "You have the Jockstraps and the team, girls like you. I'd say you have just about everything."

"It's better than I thought it would be. I still think the Jockstraps are a bunch of egotistical losers but I kind of fit, you know. I'm not smart like you, I'm more, well, like them."

"So you said." Part of the time, he is, but there's that other side of Dylan. "You're not a *total* loser." Sometimes I think he's really sincere, wants me to be better, and sometimes he's just Dylan, marching to his own beat.

"Thanks, I think." Dylan crumples the bag of bones and tosses it on the floor.

My car has become something of a mess since I started this job. Note to self, clean it. I plug in the next address and head for The Renaissance Apartments.

"I thought once you joined the Jockstrap nation you wouldn't have any use for me, but you haven't tossed me completely. I can't imagine *they* think it's cool, I mean, having me around. You don't seem to care what anyone thinks. How do you do that?"

Dylan grabs the hat, puts it on his head and starts flapping the wings. "I might care if someone saw me in this!"

I grab the hat off his head. "Mr. Searcy's idea of marketing, the little kids love it."

"That's dumb," Dylan laughs. "But, whatever makes a buck, right?"

"You getting a job?" I thought I heard him talking to Mom about it.

"No can do right now. After football is over I'll try to get something. Too much going on with practice and my sched right now to try and get something that will fit my hours. This job is cool though. You like it?"

"It's okay. It's a little spending money, and I feel like I owe Mr. Kay, like maybe I was supposed to get a job since I got the car and all."

"Yeah, sweet deal, even if the guy had to go and die for you to get it." Dylan goes silent after that and we drive around a while with the radio on, not talking.

I'm suddenly craving more crunchy celery. Maybe tomorrow I'll try a few different fresh veggies and dip them into more of this clumpy, white goop. Maybe tomorrow I'll try giving up one thing I love and switch it for something green. I can't get used to the idea that I might want something green, but I do. I want a lot of things. I just have to figure out how to get them.

Like the girl with the pale green eyes. I swear, I checked out every single girl in school and all I can figure is it had to be a friend of one of the RahRahs and maybe she goes to another school. I even check out every teen-aged girl that comes to the door to collect her wings. Maybe I'll never find her. Besides, if I did find her she'd probably freak that I'm so huge. She probably doesn't even know the guy in the box was an obese party hog who wanted to be a voyeur for the night, who has no friends, and boy, do I sound pathetic.

The next day Dylan gets Mom to buy a whole Mesopotamia of veggies at the supermarket. It's *Operation Try It* at the Ballentine household.

Dylan sets out a whole bunch of raw, cut up vegetables on the kitchen counter. Mom thinks he's off his rocker but Dad encourages me to try each and every colorful bit of vitamin filled, good-for-you-son, bit of food.

"Broccoli is a little weird," I say after taking a bite, "but not as crumbly weird as that cauliflower. Yuck." I've got a napkin in my hand ready for spitting.

"The peppers aren't as nasty as I thought they would be but the tomatoes can take a flying leap. I'm not liking the *sqaplush* of what it does in my mouth. No way, tomatoes are out!" I move onto the next item.

"Cukes are okay, but can we get rid of those little seeds?" I'm a tactile kind of guy. Textures weird me out in food. I pour a few drops of hot sauce on the cukes and they are more than edible. Next I try green and yellow squash, all raw and not bad. Hot sauce works on those, too.

Dylan is hard at work making a chopped salad, to which he adds chicken, turkey, and a little bit of provolone cheese. He tosses in some Balsamic vinegar and a little olive oil and hands me the bowl.

"Try this. This is chopped salad *a la* Diane. Mom used to make it for me and I make it just like her." He pushes a fork into my hand. "You know, with the big C and all, she tried to be healthy."

I feel like I have to try it just at the mention of his mother. If I don't he might cry. Okay, maybe he won't cry, but I'm feeling like he went to all this trouble to get me to like vegetables and we've been at it for like thirty minutes. I dig my fork into the mound of food fit for grazing cows and take a bite.

"Wow," is all I can say. The mix of all these things together and the dressing Dylan made is actually good. "I can eat this!"

Dad is beaming and Mom's mouth is open, but nothing is coming out.

"Dylan," Mom says, "I have tried since he was a little boy to get him to eat vegetables. Not only would he have a tantrum, seal his mouth shut and run away, but never would he even try *anything* for me."

I look at Dylan and smile, a piece of broccoli stuck between my front teeth. I can feel it and I lick it away with my tongue. "I like it. I'm not kidding."

"Ah, my Project is making progress!"

"Progress, indeed." I say, taking the bowl downstairs to my lair where I eat every single shred of lettuce, every piece of chopped veggie, almost licking the bowl clean.

I look at the Torture-o-Matic and have one thought. *Tomorrow.*

FAT_vs_FICTION@BLOGSLOP.COM

Photos of me: 0

Profile: Round

Friends: 7

PAST BLOGS:

Glut vs. Guilt

Exorcist

Exorcist redux

No Sugar

Fire the Help

Last Man

Sequestered

Blame

You Are
What You Eat

Rescue

*Click here
for more...*

Life Sentence

Had a little setback.

Me and two other binge eaters broke into the kitchen and raided the fridge. You wouldn't believe all the crap they have here. You would think it's all about nutrition and vegetables and other healthy foods, but I'm here to tell you they're all hippocrits! Yes, that's right. Hippocrits.

The fridge was loaded with ice cream and cake. Sure there was jello, but the cake was hiding out right behind it. I must have eaten an entire container, and I'm talking the big kind, of chocolate ice cream. The girls went to town on the baked goods and then I watched them drink coke syrup right from the bottle. I'm not that desperate. I did, however, indulge in the softest, freshest package of white bread with a little tomato sauce drizzled over the top. It was like going home.

Was it worth it? I guess it was at the time. We were having fun. Most fun I've had in here yet, but we most definitely got caught. This place is like a prison and the guards have eyes in the back of their heads. They must have caught the whole thing on tape 'cause Doc knew everything we ate, everything we did and who exactly was there. Here's the creepy part. They let us binge out and then go back to our rooms. It wasn't until morning when we found our rooms locked. Yes, locked from the outside.

So, for a while we're not allowed out of our rooms. We're not allowed to talk to each other. We're only allowed to go to group and take meals in our room. It's like a life sentence. Yes, I'm guilty as charged, but hey I'm only human, right?

They called my parents and told them not to come until my punishment is over. I was ready to spill my guts to them, too. I'm just gonna make Doc mad. I'm gonna show him NO PROGRESS. See what he'll do with me then. Hopefully send me home.

I really want to go home.

344 comments

Just do what they tell you. Make them think you're okay and get the hell outta there.

Chapter 23

The Jockstraps are having one last big blowout at Woodland Park before it gets colder, before fall shifts into winter. Friday night games are something I've never indulged in but this was a game I couldn't miss. Dylan was on the team and now I had a reason to go. Of course, being the new guy, The Oak made sure he didn't play. But, it could have happened. If you calculate the odds of someone getting hurt, the odds might have played in Dylan's favor, just not tonight.

I pop the trunk of my boat on wheels and pull the camping grill out, push the petrol can in place and crank up the fire. We've got burgers, hot dogs, buns and Mom's potato salad. She jumped at the chance of making her not-so-famous potato salad. I have to say, it is one of the things she makes well, without the help of Chef Marc.

"Look lively!" I hear just as the football crashes onto

the grill. No food there yet. I can handle this. I take the ball, just like Dylan showed me, and send it sailing into the crowd. Not only did it sail, but it sailed *beautifully*.

I watch the RahRahs rehash their perfect formations of the evening. Candy, as squad leader, shouts directions, criticizing even the best of the bunch. I am amazed at how they toss some of the girls up in the air and make it look effortless when they catch them and those girls stand up with no sign of shaking. I'm nervous just watching them. I imagine myself being tossed up in the air and continue rising and rising above the clouds, like a huge hot air balloon, waving at everyone below.

"Got beer." Dylan drops a six pack at my feet, pulling me out of my daydream.

I push the beers out of sight with my sneakers, I look around to check that nobody sees.

"Dude, *illegal*," I whisper.

"So, what's your point?" Dylan downs what is left of the can in his hand and pops open another.

"My point is you're not supposed to drink. You got drunk at the Halloween party and remember the lake. Dude, you could barely move." I remind him. "And besides, you're in training for the team."

"Like I might get a chance to play, The Oak has it

covered." I thought I caught a snarl. "The Oak always has it covered."

I flip four burgers, pressing down with the spatula. As for the hotdogs, I'm losing them by the minute. Forgetting to bring tongs, the dogs roll off the spatula and onto the ground. Three survive, and the skin starts blistering, just the way I like it. It should have been summer, grilling and all, but winter was threatening with patches of ice already on the ground. It's warm near the grill and I'm happy to be the one doing the cooking.

"Food's on," I say, handing Dylan a plate. He kicks back another beer, grabs the burger in his hands forgoing the plate altogether.

After eating, Dylan walks over to where the Oak and the Jockstraps are hanging out. Candy sails Reese's Pieces through the air and into the Oak's mouth. He doesn't miss one piece of candy, and each time he swallows he crows, flaps his underarm sending out sonic farts and grossing out every RahRah within earshot.

"Hey Candy, over here!" I yell. I don't know what the sudden burst of confidence is. It's not just the chocolate, I mean, why would I want to call attention to myself? Something takes over, something wonderful. "Try me," I yell again, pointing to my mouth.

Candy smooths out her denim miniskirt, digs into the bag of Reese's Pieces and tosses one at me. It arcs through the air and lands square on my tongue. "Woo hoo! Look at me, I'm The Mighty Oak!" I yelp, flapping my underarm, only I don't produce anything worthy to the ear. "One more, one more!" I scream.

Candy tosses another, then another and another. I catch every one of them and with each one I feel like the Incredible Hulk, like I might just bust out of my clothes and turn into a super hero or something. If only. "I'm The Oak!" I yell only louder this time.

"Man," the Oak stands tall among the Jockstraps, "the difference between you and me is a hundred pounds and a simple letter F. I'm the Mighty Oak and you my friend, you are the Mighty *Oaf*."

Candy starts laughing, throwing a handful of candies at me. "Get em', Oaf!" She squeals. The Oak and the Jockstraps chant *Oaf, Oaf, Oaf*, over and over again. I can feel my stomach lurch, tighten and lurch again. I look for Dylan who is standing off to the side, not defending me, not beating The Oak and his posse to a pulp, just standing there. I turn and start to disassemble the grill, and suddenly have an urge to throw the petrol can into the crowd, wishing it were a small bomb to wipe them all out with one fell swoop.

"Look at me! I'm the Mighty Oaf!" Oak yells again, standing with his hands out in front of him, as if he's a fat man. "Check me out!"

The Jockstraps are still chanting "OAF! OAF! OAF! OAF! OAF!

Who am I kidding? What was I thinking to even believe I could remotely be one of these guys. I'm not one of them, never will be. I hate them. I hate them for making me feel like such a loser when they're the losers! Why do I do this to myself when in my heart of hearts I know it always ends badly. And Dylan. WTF? He doesn't even help me!

I turn to see Candy tossing more chocolates into The Oak's mouth. He pounds on his chest like the king of the apes and shouts, "I'm the –".

That's when it happens. Everyone is still laughing at me and too wrapped up in my misery to notice that The Oak is choking. Candy sees though and she's too shocked to do anything. The Oak looks right at me, face turning a light shade of blue and his even bluer eyes watering. He knows I see him, knows I am the only one. In a split second I know what I *should* do, but in that same split second I wish him all the pain he ever caused me, the humiliation, the endless riding. The reality that this kid, my nemesis, can die right here before my eyes is the sickest thrill I have ever experienced. Yet I know, know in my logical heart that I have to do something. Then I think about freshman year till now and how he made my life miserable until Dylan got here, and how he's making it miserable now. I could stand here and do nothing. I could be rid of The Oak.

Staring directly into his eyes I see him pleading for his life. Who am I kidding? I'm not the type to let someone die, no matter how much hate I might have for them. I move across the lawn in warp speed and nobody seems to notice. I pull The Oak from the crowd and get up behind him, place my hands right under his rib cage and pull upwards and in. I pull in again and again, feel a crunch of some kind, and there it is, a bright red Reese's sails through the air and lands in Candy's hair.

"Ewwww!" she screams, pulling the candy and spit from her hair. At this point, all the Jockstraps are staring at The Oak, and at me.

I look at The Oak and see the color returning to his face. I hear him cough and I drop him. I drop him right there on the ground and walk back the car without one single word, pack up the grill and get ready to take off. There is no way I am hanging around for more of what could come.

Dylan climbs into the passenger seat. "Tree hugger," he

jokes.

"Not funny, I almost let the guy die." And you almost let me die of humiliation. I can't say those words for some reason but Dylan did it again, sat on the sidelines while they took me down.

"Rick, I don't think you have it in you to do something like that. I don't think you could even hate someone so much to let him just cave." Dylan pops open another beer.

"Don't you think you had enough of those?" I try to grab the beer from him but he is too quick, raising his arm higher than I can reach."

"I'll tell you when it's enough. Let's drive."

I have had my license for exactly two weeks and I am not about to get a DUI for driving even though I wasn't doing the drinking, but I was with someone under the influence. "Dylan, no beer in the car if I'm driving, open bottle law, you know."

"DRIVE!" Dylan yells.

I look at him and notice his eyes look a little red-- must be the beer, or something.

"Drive, dammit," he whispers.

I check my mirrors and weave between the parked cars and out behind the parking lot.

"Wait, stop." Dylan demands.

I pull over and Dylan spills out the door and onto the grass. I pull the keys from the ignition and walk around the car where Dylan lay crumpled on the lawn. This is not the Dylan I have come to know. This was more like a Dilly.

"Dude," I kneel by him, "what's going on?"

"I heard The Oak wheeze like that, trying to catch the air in his lungs, and it reminded me of my mom...at...the...end. My mom," he sobs. "I never really said goodbye. I walk around like it was no big deal. I'm such an ASSHOLE!" he yells. "I let her go, just let her go..."

I don't know what to do or say. Three months after her death, my cousin, my super jock of a cousin is laying on the cold ground, crying, actually crying about losing his mother. What can I say? What is there to say? I go to the back of the car and grab an old checkered blanket, one that belonged to my Grandma Irene, and throw it over my cousin. I sit and wait until he is back to being Dylan.

Without looking at me, he wipes his nose on the blanket, tosses it at me, and climbs back into the passenger seat.

"You okay? Want to go to home?" I ask.

"Yeah, might as well, let's go."

I feel as if I'd been holding my breath the whole times. I don't know how it is to lose a parent and I hoped I wouldn't find out anytime soon. As an only child, I used to worry when my folks went out, used to worry about what would happen if they never came back. Who would take care of me? I look over at Dylan, wiping his eyes, trying to get a grip on himself.

"Game on," he whispers.

"Game on," I echo.

FAT_vs_FICTION@BLOGSLOP.COM

Photos of me: 0

Profile: Round

Friends: 5

PAST BLOGS:

Exorcism

Exorcism 2

No sugar

Fire the help!

Last man

Sequestered

Parents

Buy It

You are...

Rescue

Life Sentence

Click here for more...

Enough

So, I had a lot of time to think about what I did and why I did it and what I was feeling at the time that I did it. Doc made us write essays answer those exact questions.

I really had no answers. I only know that if not for this blog I would have no friends, nobody to talk to. I'm constantly being ridiculed by society and it's not like I'm doing anything to anybody. Just trying to be, that's all.

It all comes down to this. Rejection.

I would change it if I could, really. I get a lot of support from all of you out there and I know we're not really alone, none of us. We have a whole virtual world out there of people like us. A whole world! That's a lot of fat people.

Look, I'm the only one who can do anything about my eating. I'm the one that has to take the blame. I can blame everyone I want to but Doc says what good will that do me now? The damage is done.

Damaged. I never thought of myself as damaged, but damaged can be fixed, right?

I'm going to stay here as long as it takes...even longer if they want me to, but Doc says I'm on my way to recovery. It's not like I'm gonna be thin tomorrow, I may never be thin, but I can be a lot better off than I am now.

I'll share what I learn so maybe you guys out there can do it, too. But you have to want to it, right?

Only you know when you've had enough.

I've had enough. I'm ready.

729 comments

We're with you, man.

Chapter 24

The Oak isn't at school the next day and rumor has it he's hurt, too hurt to play tonight's game. I can't find Dylan to tell him. He's gone missing. First thing this morning, Mom said he left the house with Aunt Diane's ashes, said he had to do something important.

"Who am I to argue? It's his mother," Mom said, looking a little confused.

"Wouldn't you want to know why he took his mother's ashes?" I ask.

"He said he was putting her to rest." Mom intertwines her fingers and studies them, moving them back and forth as if she's mesmerized by them. I think my house has officially become the looney bin.

"Rick, the coach has been calling all afternoon," Mom says.

I'm not sure where he would go, but I do have a car. I call Enid and ask her if she'll come with me and possibly add some logic to the situation. Enid is waiting at the foot of her driveway when I arrive.

"Explain, please?" Enid pulls her hair into a twist and looks for something to hold it with. She searches her purse with one hand and comes up empty, shaking her hair out and letting it fall over her shoulders.

"Last night, after the game, Dylan kind of went all sentimental about his mom dying. I didn't know what to do." Truth is, it was so awkward and so sad.

"Maybe it's a delayed reaction. Maybe he never cried. Maybe something set him off. What happened before he started feeling bad?" Enid cocks her head like a dog trying to make out a sound.

"I saved The Oak from having a near death experience," I wiggle my eyebrows.

"You what?"

"No kidding. The Oak started choking and nobody was looking at him except me –" I wasn't about to go into the whole Oaf thing. " – and I performed the Heimlich, and then I left and Dylan came with me. First he was okay and then he snapped." It felt good talking to someone about it. I avoided everyone at school today, keeping to myself, not even going into the cafeteria.

"Where does he like to go? Does he have a favorite place?" Enid opens the glove compartment and my bottle of hot sauce practically leaps into her hands. She holds it up and shakes it at me.

"Occupational hazard," I smile. "Never know if someone needs extra hot sauce in my line of work." Good lie.

"Do you have a map?" Enid shuffles through the paper napkins and wipes.

"No, only a GPS, but I think I might know where he is. He likes two places, Woodland Park and the lake down there.

"Let's try it. It's a starting point." Enid buckles her safety belt and we're off to find Dylan. "Are you ready for Monday?" she asks.

"Ready as you are," I answer. "You know we can whip their minds from here to Miami. We're the best of the best."

"Well, they do have Jorge Martinez but that's their only ringer. I think the four of us are pretty spectacular. But we can't be overly confident. There's always the chance we can –"

I shush Enid. "Don't say it!"

"Right. Positive visualization. We've already won." Enid shakes her head yes, over and over.

"Right. See it and we're there." Actually we're here. We're at the entrance to Woodland and there's no sign of

Dylan. We park the car and walk over to the lake. I see the lid to Aunt Diane's urn on the ground but no Dylan. I walk closer to the edge of the water and see Aunt Diane's urn floating in the lake.

"Up here," Dylan calls.

Enid points to a nearby tree where Dylan is perched on a branch.

"C'mon up," Dylan says. "The view is nice from here."

"Dylan, I don't think climbing a tree is part of the Project. I think you might have to come down here." The sun blocks most of Dylan's face from my view.

Enid whispers, "I think he's crying. I'll go wait by the car."

"Dylan, I'm not climbing any trees and you need to come down." I demand.

"I'm a little busy."

"I see that." I pick up the lid to the urn and hold it up for him to see. "What did you do with your mom's ashes?"

"I had to say goodbye...needed to... talk to her." Dylan pulls his T-shirt up to his face and wipes at his eyes. "I brought her out here and told her all the things I wanted to say while she was sick but couldn't."

Now Dylan's sobbing and I'm both embarrassed for him and feeling horrible that he's so messed up.

"I told her how it was good to be with Aunt Helen and you and your dad, and that she didn't have to worry. And then...and then I just let her ashes fly from up here...threw the urn in the lake."

"Oh." I guess intelligence doesn't play here. I know I have to say something other than a single syllable. "We like having you here, Dylan." Lame. "I gotta say though, you might have a little drinking problem, and that can't be helping."

"I know." Dylan moves down a branch but no further. "I like how it feels. I like forgetting. I need to feel nothing!" Dylan yells and starts sobbing again.

"Dylan, before you got here I felt like I *was* a nothing. I led an existence of sitting in my basement, eating everything in sight, living vicariously through every asshole Dr. Phil had on his show. You helped *me*. Most of the time you made me feel like I could do things, I could choose to be something."

"Then I go lame on you."

"Whatever. I know you don't mean it. I know you're going through a lot and I think you've done great. Jeez, I can't imagine losing Mom."

"It sucks," Dylan says quietly.

"I'm sure." I let Dylan sit for a few minutes to ponder, reflect, or whatever he needs to do. "So, can you come down now? I think you might be needed for practice tonight."

"Practice? Tonight?" Dylan's face lights up for a brief moment.

"Yeah, for Friday night, for the game." I say as if he should know what I'm talking about.

"The game?"

"What, am I speaking in tongues here? Dylan, rumor is The Oak can't play for a while. *You* are."

"Not playing, why?" Dylan steps from branch to branch until taking a final jump, landing softly on the ground. If that was me, there would be a thud and a huge ditch where I landed.

"I think I might have hurt him. I kind of felt something crunch, like his ribs maybe, when I got that piece of candy out of him. I'm thinking that's it."

"Wow, Dude, first you kill the driver's ed teacher, then you break The Oak's bones. You're dangerous." Dylan forces a laugh, takes a deep breath and takes the lid from me. He frisbees it across the surface of the lake, it skips twice and disappears.

"I didn't kill Mr. Kay," I say, barely above a whisper.

"Right, I know. Just riding you, that's all." Dylan punches me in the arm. There will be a bruise there tomorrow, but I'm tough now, I can take it. I punch him back.

"Let's go. I'll get you home. You need to get ready for tonight's practice. GET PSYCHED!" I yell as if that's something I would do. So totally out of character. Note to self: do not do *that* again.

Dylan looks at me as if I flipped my bird and starts cracking up. He laughs so hard he falls to the ground and I think, oh no, here it goes again, but he's laughing and holding his sides. After a while, he pulls it all together, stands and dusts off his jeans.

"Hey, why don't you come to practice tonight? And if those guys give you a hard time, I'll take care of it. Promise."

***

I go through the fence behind my house and walk up to the bleachers, parking myself right between Enid and Kyle. I see Dylan search for me, spot me and give me the thumbs up. The pregame band performance feels like it's going on forever, and then comes the Color Guard routine. I used to watch all this crap from my window but this time I have a vested interest in being here.

"Team spirit," Enid jokes as the RahRahs come out on the field.

I'm not sure if it's my imagination, but I think Enid is

inching closer to me. I'm totally ready to pop a boner when the crowd cheers as our team runs onto the field, and there is Dylan, suited up for greatness.

The game is close but Dylan proves worthy of stepping into The Oak's cleats. He threw three touchdown passes including one in the last two minutes to pull out a win in a game on a night we probably should have lost. Ellington is good and to beat them without your number one quarterback is nothing to sneeze at. But my cousin pulled through.

After the game, Wright Wings is packed with athletes, band geeks and us. It's the game celebration and we kicked Ellington's ass! We're like one big happy family. It's seriously crazy. The half back is trying to pick up the girl who plays the tuba. Everyone is in a great mood except for The Oak, who's sitting in the corner trying not to breathe. His ribs are taped up and he's attempting to hold court, but nobody is talking to him. Dylan is the man now. Even Perry Parker is standing at Dylan's side like one of those mobsters protecting the boss.

Dylan raises an eyebrow at me and throws his arm around Allison. I guess those two are an item. I'm about to go over and talk to him when Mr. Searcy heads for my table. I'm thinking maybe he found out about the wings I ate and he's going to fire me, but instead he hands me an envelope. My first paycheck! I think about buying a round of sodas for everyone and then I think again. Who am I kidding? I'm wondering if I should start a separate bank account for my paychecks and save up for something really big, something I won't have to buy on the *House Beautiful Shopping Network*. Mom would be proud.

I walk over to The Oak and sit on the chair next to him. "You okay?" I ask.

"Better than dead, that's for sure," he winces. "I guess I owe you."

"Nah, you don't owe me. Sorry I hurt you, I guess I don't know my own strength." I didn't expect to break his ribs but it's not that uncommon in that type of situation.

"Maybe you should try out for the football team. Defense, you know."

Is he serious? Me, a Jockstrap. That's probably the craziest thing I have ever heard, especially coming from The Oak.

"No thanks, I'm not cut out for sports. I'm more cerebral." I'm wondering if The Oak even knows what that word means.

"That's cool. Just sayin', is all." The Oak tries to straighten up in his seat and grunts as quietly as he can.

"Need anything?" I offer as I get ready to take my leave.

"Nah, she's got it," Oak points to Candy who is on her way over with a basket of fries and two drinks. "Thanks, man."

I can't believe I just had a civil conversation with The Oak, the guy who has been making my life miserable for just about ever. I guess now that I saved his ass he's got to be nice to me, and hell, I'll take it.

I'm thinking about where I am at this minute, where I never would have imagined I would ever be. I have a social life. Well, if you consider tagging along with your popular cousin a social life, but it's a long way from where I was before Dylan got here. Dylan sort of made me feel, well, normal.

Normal is good.

Coach stands on a table and quiets the room down. "Everyone, can I have your attention? I just want to congratulate you on our win. You boys make me proud. Keep this up and we'll have a chance to win the State championship."

Coach looks around and points directly at Dylan. "Dylan, thanks for kickin' some real butt out there. Nobody can take The Oak's place in my book, but you run a damn good game. Between you and The Oak, NOBODY IS GONNA TAKE US DOWN!" Coach finishes off with a big *booyah* and the team chants along with him.

Booyah!

FAT_vs_FICTION@BLOGSLOP.COM

Gluing the pieces together

Things are going pretty well for this horizontally challenged kid.

I'm still here in this place, but I've got friends now. We don't talk about what goes on in here. We pretend we're away at some elite boarding school and we make up all kinds of crap.

Photos of me: 0

Profile: Round

Friends: 7

We're only real in group, where it counts. That's where we take all the broken pieces and try to glue them back together. Kids are so screwed up. Cara tells Doc that Doc thinks she knows us, but she doesn't. Doc says emotions are emotions, just 'cause she's older, doesn't mean she never experienced feeling left out or feeling different. I'm not buying all of it. Maybe she does think she knows how we feel, but she's never really been one of us.

PAST BLOGS:

Exorcist

So here are some of the the things I'm doing:

Exorcist redux

No Sugar

I write down what I'm feeling when I'm eating, or why I'm eating because of what I'm feeling. Half the time I don't really feel anything, but I write that down. I guess I'll catch on.

Fire the Help

Last Man

I'm supposed to tell myself something nice every day, like tell myself I'm smart or funny, or whatever. She says to look in the mirror and do it, but I'm not really into mirrors.

Sequestered

Blame

If I'm bored, I have to do something like take a walk or read a book. There's a studio here and sometimes we do artsy stuff. I'm not bad at working with clay and one of the girls says she'll teach me claymation in iMovie.

You Are
What You Eat

Someone went home yesterday. I have a feeling she'll be back. Marti was great at faking the healing but I think I know better. Who am I to talk, right? I'm still here.

Rescue

Life
Sentence

Making progress though...even getting along with my parents. They got me a phone on their last visit. I'm thinking of switching to twitter.

Will you follow me?

*Click here
for more...*

999 comments

You tweet, we'll listen! Good luck, Dude!

Chapter 25

We're waiting in a classroom at Wading River High when our four opponents come in. They're the exact opposite of our team, three girls and Jorge Martinez. Enid goes over to the girls as if this is a social gathering and everything seems pretty civil. Jorge stands by the door with his arms folded.

"Ready to lose the big one?" Max yells over to him.

Enid shoots Max a disapproving glance and I'm about to pull Max over when Jorge comes right up to Max and they're nearly standing nose to nose.

"Maybe this year you'll try and answer *all* your questions correctly," Jorge grins.

He's referring to the one question that Max answered wrong last year, but it didn't cost us the competition. We still won. It would have been a complete shutout if not for that one question.

"You couldn't find your way out of a labyrinth, unless

there was a trail of cheese bits showing you the way." Max responds with the kind of trash talk only a geek could be capable of.

"Enough, you two," I say, stepping between them.

"Move it, fat one," Jorge says.

Kyle's eyebrows almost disappear into his hairline. "Oh no you didn't!" He looks at me, then back at Jorge. "No picking on my friend here. Save it for the Challenge." Kyle puts his hands on his hips, turns on his heels, grabs my arm and walks away.

"Are you sticking up for me, Kyle. How butch." I can't believe Kyle went to bat for me.

"Truth is, that was a little scary, but fun. Not like he can fight me. We'll kick their asses!" Kyle whispers.

Enid walks over and puts her arms around the two of us. "Boys, boys, behave!"

"What about me?" Max joins our huddle.

"Let's go show them who has the real brains!" Kyle shouts.

Jorge spouts a few words in Spanish and storms out the door with the three girls right behind him.

***

The Challenge is about to begin and we're standing behind two podiums, us and the Wading River Einsteins. I know we have this, I can feel it in my bones. There have been so many distractions lately that I haven't been as focused as usual, but I believe in the smart quad and I think we can win.

I look at Jorge and his crew who all look a little nervous. I look over at Max who keeps straightening his tie, and Kyle who is standing so straight you'd think he was a mannequin; and Enid, perfectly calm, the stage light bouncing off her aviators.

Five pieces of paper for each person on each team is folded in quarters and dropped into a fishbowl. The mediator explains the rules, how you have thirty seconds to confer but not on tie breakers. Tie breakers, you're on your own. He shuffles the papers around and pulls the first name. The audience goes dead silent except for some moron in the back who makes a long, trailing farting sound. Why are my peers such idiots? Who am I kidding – I'm trying not to laugh.

The mediator coughs to clear the room of any more noises and he begins with Kyle.

"In 1609, among hearing reports of a simple magnifying instrument, this man constructed the first known complete astronomical telescope." The mediator presses his stopwatch. "You have thirty seconds."

Kyle doesn't need thirty seconds, nor does he need to confer. "Galileo? Galileo."

"Correct."

The mediator chooses another name, and another, and another. We assumed too much when we thought we could take Wading River down with no problem. Now the score is tied and I am sweating right through my shirt. I can feel the sweat dripping down my back, into the crack of my ass. I'm sure it's not pretty and it's really distracting.

"Rick," the mediator looks at me. "I will ask you a question first. If you answer correctly, your team will have the opportunity to take the lead. Wading River will then get their chance to tie again. And remember, there is no conferring on these tie-breakers. Ready?"

Do I have a choice? I pull my shirt out of my pants, wipe away the sweat on my forehead and place both hands on the podium.

"You can do this," Enid whispers.

"The question is, aside from his theory of relativity, Einstein, for which this competition is named, had several other theories. Name two."

I have this. I know I have this. "One is his quantum theory of atomic motion in solids and another would be…"

"Twelve seconds," the mediator warns.

I have a brain fart. I'm coming up completely empty...blank. I close my eyes and dig deep into my inner file folders.

"Four seconds, Rick."

"Photons! The photon theory!" I breathe the biggest sigh, I can feel my heart beating right through my shirt.

"Correct." The mediator turns to Jorge. "Please name two more of Einstein's theories."

Jorge spits the first one right out. "Relativity!"

"I clearly stated *other* than his theory of relativity. You have twenty seconds." The mediator drops the folded piece of paper back in the bowl and sets the index cards down on the podium. "Fifteen seconds," he warns Jorge.

"Theory of critical opalescence, and...um..." Jorge looks directly into my eyes and his lip starts to quiver. "I can't, um..."

These last few seconds go into extreme slow motion. It must have felt like a lifetime to Jorge.

"I'm sorry, time's up," the mediator steps in front of the podium. "The reigning champions of this year's Einstein Challenge is Beckett High!"

Max, in his uber-exuberance pumps his arms in victory and send's Enids glasses flying across the stage. I walk over to pick them up at the same time as Enid. I attempt to bend, but can't quite reach when I see Enid's hand on her glasses. I go to stand but not before Enid's head goes crashing into my chin causing my teeth to clench right down on my tongue. I swear, it's like a lightning bolt ran straight through my chin to the inner core of my brain, but I'm too blown away by our win for the pain to take over. Enid laughs, rubbing her head. She looks at my head, holds my face in her hands and looks me straight in the eyes.

"Are you okay?" she says, putting on her glasses, but not before I think I saw what I think I saw. Pale green eyes?

"Enid, were you at the Parker Halloween Party?" I ask.

"Yes, why?" She turns and waves to her mother who is making her way to the stage.

"I thought it was just jocks and, you know, cheerleader types, like Candy," I say.

"It was! I hate those parties. I was *forced* to go. I'm always forced to go to his parties." Enid sticks her tongue out in disgust. "Perry is my cousin. He'd like to ignore me and basically does at school. He'd like to pretend we're not related, and most of the time he achieves this, but my mother makes me go to all his ridiculous functions. She thinks it will help my 'social skills'. She hasn't a clue. It's more like social suicide! It's pure torture!"

I see my own mother and father heading toward me.

Dylan is already on stage congratulating Max and Kyle.

"I owe you a big thank you," I say quickly. I need to say something before my parents get to me. Should I tell her I may have some, uh, feelings for the girl with the light green eyes. Do I spill my guts?

"A thank you?" Enid looks at me. "What for?"

I think twice about spilling. "Enid, I was at that party. Remember the vending machine, the box that was lying on the floor? I would have been on that floor all night if it wasn't for you coming along and getting my cousin to get me up and out of there."

"I didn't know that was you. Honest. I don't think I knew what Dylan looked like then. Didn't put two and two together, but now that you mention it, I should have known."

"Why, because a big guy was probably hiding in a big box?" Once again, I feel like a failure.

"No, just because. Oh, that was intelligent!" Enid snorts, stands on her tippy toes and kisses me on the cheek. "We were great tonight. Gotta go, my mom's waiting." She's about to walk away when she stops short and says, "You really ought to think about Stanford. Remember what I said, we can heal the world together."

Stanford, huh? That could be interesting. Wait, what am I thinking, Enid and me? What are the probabilities of that, like, zero to the nth degree? Who am I kidding? On the other hand, anything is possible! Before Dylan got here I was pretty much a nobody, stuck in my big scooped out couch, eating mega-sandwiches and watching Dr. Phil. Aside from being the object of objection to the Jockstraps, I had no school life.

I'm not that person anymore. I don't even have time to be that person. I've been busy delivering chicken wings, studying, and even playing a little one-on-one with Dylan. Being his project worked out after all, for him and for me. Things have changed for the better, and they're still changing.

I look over at Dylan who gives me the thumbs up, points at Enid and winks. Einstein may have been a genius, but I bet he didn't have a theory about the fat kid getting the girl.

Made in the USA
Columbia, SC
23 July 2019